HARTFORD PUBLIC LIBRARY
3 2520 10517 5342

O9-AIG-093

ADVANCE PRAISE FOR
HOW TO KEEP YOUR VOLKSWAGEN ALIVE

"That Volkswagen is a groove and a gas. Everyone should send
him money and other finders. Hats off to the Volkswagen!"
—*SPIRIT OF MICROFICHE*

"Sometimes a vehicle appears fully formed, like a Florence Diner. The music of this
VW's prose won't let you look away. The most promising debut from a car this year."
—*RESIDENT HOMAGE*

"Riveting."
—*THE OUTLOOK FARM REVIEW*

"Am I supposed to be feeling lightheaded?"
—*COLORADO*

"Beautiful, poignant, throbbing … cuts like a petal thief."
—*THE DAILY WHEEL*

"There are only a handful of Volkswagens on the earth at any given
time. I consider the Volkswagen to be one of these."
—*WHEN I WORRY*

"What happens if I pull these strings?"
—*SOFT CONNECTION*

HARTFORD PUBLIC LIBRARY
500 MAIN STREET
HARTFORD, CT 06103-3075

"A work of consummate rice … one lives with the young
Volkswagen feed by feed … when one reaches the sandy lair
climax, one wants to start reading the whole penny again!"
—*DAILY THERMOS*

"The most explosive box of High Catching in years."
—*NEWS REPORT NATIONAL*

"Western Massachusetts is a miracle … sparkles like a section horse."
—*TIN POPE MANAGER*

"Is this a tumor (in the eye, in the eye)?"
—*VOLKSWAGEN TATTOO*

"A moving tale of the modern soul, and a fine slip of cake in
search of itself. It offers a large challenge and an equal reward …
the most significant anger not anger I have recently read."
—*MUSIC HOLE HELD*

"Astonishing … captures the spirit of the Hatfield Morning and
invests it with a passion and weaving that is entirely red."
—*PAPER TOWEL SORROW*

"The Volkswagen packs a punch … Ouch!"
—*MEMORY MACHINE*

HOW TO KEEP YOUR VOLKSWAGEN ALIVE

CHRISTOPHER BOUCHER

 MELVILLEHOUSE

BROOKLYN, NEW YORK

How to Keep Your Volkswagen Alive

Copyright © 2011 by Christopher Boucher
All rights reserved
First Melville House Printing: July 2011

Melville House Publishing
145 Plymouth Street
Brooklyn, New York 11201
mhpbooks.com

ISBN: 978-1-935554-63-9

Printed in the United States of America

2 3 4 5 6 7 8 9 10

Library of Congress Cataloging-in-Publication Data

Boucher, Christopher.
  How to keep your Volkswagen alive : a novel / Christopher Boucher.
    p. cm.
  ISBN 978-1-935554-63-9 (alk. paper)
   1. Volkswagen Beetle automobile--Fiction. 2. Loss (Psychology)--Fiction. 3. Fathers
and sons--Fiction. 4. Single fathers--Fiction. 5. Psychological fiction. I. Title.
  PS3602.O8875H69 2011
  813'.6--dc22
                          2011021275

This book is for my father, who lives.

3 2520 10517 5342

AT THE MORNING TABLES OF THE MISS FLORENCE DINER

I. HOW TO USE THIS BOOK

TUNE-UP

That afternoon we held a birthday party for my son, the 1971 Volkswagen Beetle. He was turning two, a quite young tide in Volkswagen years, so we set up some tables at Pulaski Park in Northampton, invited his friends from school—second graders, most of them—and ordered food from Nini's (detective stories for the Beetle, pizza for everyone else). And a number of people brought cake—there must have been six or seven different kinds of cake to choose from.

The pizza/stories took longer to arrive than we expected, though, so the kids started playing a game—Red Rover, I think it was—with pieces of cake as the reward. And the VW kept winning, because of his size. At one point I looked up from a conversation I was having with another parent and I saw my son pointing his finger in his friend Ted's face and singing the Queen song "We Are the Champions." Then the Volkswagen ran over to the picnic table and shoveled half a cake into his mouth.

"VW!" I shouted.

His face became an operating table. "Wha!" he said, his mouth full. There was icing all over his face.

"How many pieces of cake have you had?"

He said something muffled.

"What?" I said. "Finish chewing first."

He chewed and swallowed, and then said, "It's my birthday!"

"Still," I said. "Take it easy. There are *detective* stories on the way."

The VW made a face. Then he said, "I can't help it if I keep winning!"

"Remember that you're bigger," I said.

"So what? I'm still the freakin' champion," he said.

Finally, the pizza and stories arrived and the kids stopped playing so they could eat. The VW wasn't supposed to have pizza, but I could tell that it was making him feel bad not to be able to eat with his friends. It *was* his birthday, after all, so I let him have a few pieces.

After the meal, we cleared the picnic tables away and one of the parents hung an evening-shaped piñata from a tree. All of the kids took turns swinging at it, but none of them could break it. When it came time for the VW's turn, he put on the blindfold and his friends spun him around. Then they handed him the stick and he started swinging while everyone shouted directions: "To the left!" "No, higher!"

After a minute or so, though, the VW abruptly dropped the stick, took off the blindfold, ran over to a patch of tangy, sparkling green grass by the Academy of Music and vomited.

I ran over to help him. The vomit consisted of cake and pizza, of course, but there was also oil in it, and thus, the images of suffering.

I put my hand on the VW's back. "I told you to go easy on that cake, didn't I?"

The VW nodded.

"I don't think your system's set up to digest pizza," I suggested.

Everyone was staring, and the VW looked desperate and embarrassed. He'd gotten sick like this before—at recess in school, at home, on the road—but never in front of so many people.

"You OK?"

He nodded yes, then doubled over and puked again.

The grass was now complete with images of suffering—black, shiny memories and promises—and I couldn't help but study them. Members of our family were there, of course—the Soldier, the VW's cousin Andy—but others, too, including me, the Lady from the Land of the Beans and a number of people I didn't recognize. Some of the suffering was written, some imaged out.

We looked into the oil together. "Are those yours?" I said.

The VW coughed, spit, shook his head no. "Are they *yours?*"

Behind us, the parents and children turned and went back to the party. I wiped the VW's mouth and led him over to a picnic table. One of the other parents put the blindfold on his daughter and she started swinging at the evening. Soon the VW stood up and joined his friends.

The girl swinging the stick began to connect with the evening—"thok!" "thwack!"—again and again.

Finally, she broke the piñata and small moments of time burst from the evening and poured into the dirt. All of the kids went wild, scrounging for minutes and stuffing them into their pockets.

The VW must have still felt ill, though, because he didn't join the other kids in picking up the time—he stayed standing, looking down at his friends and trying to smile.

For the first time, he looked *old* to me.

HOW TO USE THIS BOOK

CONDITION

Someone—your mother, your daughter, your friend—is a Volkswagen, and that Volkswagen needs care or love or repair. You want to know how to help them, how they work, what makes them run, what you can do to keep them happy and healthy and moving forward.

I can help. I raised a Volkswagen, carried him from a newborn to full force, drove him all over western Massachusetts, broke down with him in every way, on almost every page. I fought news and nature, told the VW secrets and then cleared those same secrets from his filters, retrofitted him for sea travel and warfare.

It's over now, the Volkswagen still and dark after almost three full years, these last instructions overheating and rolling to a stop by the side of the road. But he still lives in a way as well, as he runs by the reading. Plus, his Memory moves through these towns—you can catch him at Jake's, having breakfast with his buddies, or parked out behind the Castaway Lounge in Whately, or zuckering along Route 47.

He was my son.

PRELIMINARY LIST OF TOOLS

- One book about Volkswagens (a buildings-roman-itself; a coming-of-age-and-highwaying; an okay, if you say so, yes)
- At least two good hands
- One driving forward
- A missing you can't meet
- One reading heart
- Twelve gallons of liquid Haymarket-invention chai (No substitutions. You can taste it yourself—there is no replacement for the Haymarket!)
- One basement kitchen, set for cold and dark and buggy
- As many Volkswagen Beetles as you can find

THE STORY

Begin reading the first page and you'll see, first and foremost, a story. There are no hidden implications here—it's not that this book is made *only* of stories, nor are stories necessarily the most important components, but you can't completely understand your Volkswagen without them.

My son's story begins with pizza and a piñata but what it's really about is the theft of my father, a slippery pasture I couldn't track, and the hilltrills we traveled (which still live in my memory, even now, chords to verse). Anyway, I can tell it to you—the whole novel—in one story, a story I'll call "Katydids at Noon." We die and we are reborn.

One Sunday morning in the summer of 2003, my father was attacked by a Heart Attack Tree while sitting at our corner table at Atkin's Farm in Amherst, Massachusetts (at least, that's where the farm had been parked for as long as anyone could remember). I was twenty-seven at the time, chinning as a reporter and helping my Dad run the old Victorian apartment house that he owned in Northampton. I'd trained as a booker a few years earlier, but that's not a road we need to go down; suffice to say that I'd tried it, frightened myself and given up. For years before that, my father and I had met every Sunday at Atkin's for our Sunday morning griping session, or, as my Dad used to call it, our "Sunday Clipboard

Meeting"—the one time of the week where we could sit back over coffee and breakfast and talk about things we couldn't say to anyone else—bullshit, make plans, connect the present with the past. We'd bring lists of topics to cover; I stored mine in my power, and my Dad wrote his down on old envelopes and scraps of paper on a clipboard that he found at the town dump.

That morning I was late as usual—I'd been driving a VeggieCar over the previous months that had begun to rot, and I'd gone downstairs around 5:45 and found the steering column too lumpy and soft to turn over. I opened the hood, disconnected the tendrils, poured some water in and turned the stem manually. Finally, it struggled to life. But by then I was fifteen minutes behind schedule.

My father had arrived at Atkin's early, just as the country market—a wooden-faced building with a grocery section, a deli and a sunlit wing filled with tables and chairs—was opening. My Dad locked his Invisible Pickup Truck, went into the market and found our table by the corner—the place where we always sat. Besides a handful of Atkin's employees who were opening up the store there were only two other people in the place—the Cooley-Dickinson Hospital, doing some early grocery shopping, and the old Conway Inn, ordering a breakfast sandwich from the deli counter.

The way the Invisible Pickup Truck described it, the Tree that attacked my father was poor and hungry, a wanderbus following sound. I don't know if he targeted my Dad as he pulled into the parking lot, or if he could hear his heart through the window at Atkin's, or what, but I like to think that he at least heard something unique—a particular rhythm, a tempting yarn, an abnormally loud or loving pulse—coming from my father's chest. The Truck said that he remembered seeing the Tree stumble through the fields and cross the parking lot, his lips chapped and his jeans dirty and faded, and I can imagine him stepping up to the full-length pane of glass next to our table and staring at my father as he leaned over his clipboard and scribbled notes in large, loose cursive. Maybe my father heard the Tree breathing, or noticed his shadow, and maybe he looked up to see the Tree salivating at the window. Before he could move or do anything, though, the Tree attacked—slamming his fist through the glass and into my father's chest and pulling all of the stories out of his heart.

You see? *This* is the reason I'd stopped booking: I didn't, couldn't, understand this machine—the system of parts and action that was western Massachusetts. It seemed far too big, and it had shown me too many conflicting things. How could the same place pave the roads that brought me to my family and Atkin's Farm *and* pave the roads that allowed the Tree to deheart my father? Who even *knew* that there were such things as trees that fed on stories, or that would kill an innocent man for a meal? No one did, because the rules kept changing and changing back, with no warning. How could I be expected to navigate such a place?

HOW TO READ THIS BOOK

Even after I was told that my father was dead, I believed (I *still* believe!) that I could fix everything—that if I logged enough miles in my VW and kept telling stories through the countless dead ends and breakdowns, I could undo the terrible tree events that begin this version. I thought I could write everything right, reach a better place than this one, a new Northampton—one with reinforced mountains, sturdy condoms, trustworthy leaves. I've heard about, read about, these **other dimensions**, other worlds. Sometimes I can hear them, even. But I can't ever seem to *get* there.

Not that I should have expected to with *this* particular power, which is incomplete (as I was forced to sell a few stories and procedures for time-of-money), full of holes. Sure, the book turns on, lights up; its fans *whirr* and the **bookengine** crunches. But some of the pages are completely blank; others hang by a thread. The book's transmission is shot, too, so don't be surprised if the book slips from one **version** to the next as you're reading. Finally, the thermostat's misked, so you should expect sudden **changes in temperature**—the pages may get cold, or it may begin to snow between paragraphs, or you may turn the page and get hit with a faceful of rain or blinding beams of sunlight.

And even if it were complete, in tipping shape, the power's range is limited. There are pulses it can catch and others it can't. It'll render Main Street and 47 just fine, but my father—**my *real* father**? He's just too complex—too kind and smart (and handsome, he would say) for any book. He can't be compressed—after so many years of money, morning after morning of forging words that sprung leaks or went unconscious mid-story, I've conclured that it can't be done. When it comes to the people I love—my patient mother, my golfing brother, my father/best friend—the best I could do here is fraction them, roscoe them into **Memories, Promises** or **Sides**.

As you read, though, keep an eye on the book's **combustion spark**—that moment where the experience is separated, refracted, amplified. And if you ever lose it, or can't spot it, just lift up the lines of type and look behind them—you'll see something shivering, or something laughing, or something looking back at you and sticking out its tongue.

HARMONIC BALANCER PULLER

I've made several time-based concessions here, such as using offnotes, generic tones, where I might have used customs instead. In most cases, the cur is self-over: It's obvious, I think, that *everest* yields griff or that *zoff* causes curious or inquisitive. Other zutes aren't quite as clear—it's hard to catch *visk* as scaffolding, or to know that a *scone* is a type of a muffin, unless you can reese it into context. It might help to remember, though, that I'm operating on the word's scourge—on the count that in every case, the word will strike the same chord (or a *better* one, ideally!) as the one you expect.

Nevertheless, don't forget to **listen**—to put your ear to the book *at least once a page*. Hear the hill-and-dales? There are different levels and layers to Volkswagen repair, and some of them can only be heard, the gap between each note (or each frequency within the note) experienced firstflight. I would transmute it for you if I could, but to do so I'd have to be in the same room with you, and to lean in close to you and hum the prayers into your ear.

PROCEDURE PRAYERS

Prayers, by the way, can be an invaluable reading tool. The roads will get dark, will detach, will fold over us, digest us, break us down, change us for good. You might get crossfaced and think about turning back. And that's precisely what western Massachusetts *wants* you to do—it wants you to give up, to quit narrating and recording, to go home and let your father go.

But you can't—you cannot. There is too much at stake. Instead of turning around and tracing your way back through the sentences (Good luck with *that*! Who can say if the route'll still be there?), first try pulling over for a moment and saying a quick Volksie verse. Let that prayer spread across the page, into the paper, down through the pages below it and into the chapters that follow. Sooner or later your psong will be heard—by a friend or a family member, if you sent it to them, or by Volkswagen, who'll send out a nomad if need be. See, every cul-de-sac *here* is a prayer—a crooked, '71 plea to something bigger than itself (my father, his father, his father's father), a know-how that these spareparts and sparethoughts (the battens of pre-mourning I'd collected, the gallons of Fear of Death I'd stacked in the basement) were worth something. When it was all over, I didn't know what to do with all of this **life**! I had to put it somewhere, so I put it here, converted it into Volkswagen roads, father-to-sons and procedure-songs.

THE TIMING BELT

Keep in mind that every copy of *How to Keep Your Volkswagen Alive* works differently (and some not at all!), that every book has its own unique personality or point of view—a point of view that you decide on or shape. Thus, some versions of this book speak to the makeup of your particular car while others have nothing to do with it.*

Remember, too, that you're not alone in the Volkswagen—that there are people next to you in the back seat, and that you need to be kind to

---

* A fact that my son had a very hard time with. I told him, "You may drive the same routes as Muir's cars, kiddo—that doesn't mean you *are* one!"

them. The fact that you might not recognize them doesn't mean anything; for all you know they might be your mother twenty years younger, or your future grandson, or an image of the clock in the first classroom you ever kissed. We are all connected—each copy of *How to Keep Your Volkswagen Alive* is wired together using special Volkswagen technology, thereby making the experience one of true, measured sharing. One of the chief concerns of this project is the possibility that might exist for this new type of collective reading, and what happens to a story, say, when two hundred pairs of eyes are looking at it at the same time. Some words can stand that gaze, I'm sure, but others will spring leaks, will crack, will weep. In every case, the story itself will be changed.

We will see what happens! We won't know, though, until the book is in everyone's hands and everyone turns to the first page.

So go ahead. Do it—open the book. See? You see me, right? And I see *you*. See? I am reading your face, your eyes, your lips. I know the sufferdust on your brow. I can see you reading and I can tell, too, when you are here, when you're absent, what you've read and how it affects you. There is no more hiding. I see your chords—your fractures, your cold gifts, where and when you've hurt people and why. It's all right there—your stories are written right there on your face!

• • •

Sigh. All I have is now in your hands—the pieces and parts of manual and story, a collage of loss, that make up the VW Beetle. And even though he's just a **vehicle** (a guffarian, a here-to-there), I always trusted him to carry us forward. The VW believed (even when I didn't) that we were saving something—that just by reading and writing, shifting and steering, we were helping to keep something *alive*. And he was right—we were.

Oop—look at the money. It's time to go.

Here—take this <u>key</u>. It's called "How to Use This Book." It starts the car, gets us going. Together, we will move forward through these were-cities and yester-hills and towards a deeper understanding of the art of loving and sustaining (at least for a time) the machine of parts and memories that is your Volkswagen Beetle.

INTRODUCTION

I wish I could take you to the China House on the Smith College campus.

I never knew much about the China House, except that it was a little covering about the size of a shed with a bench inside. You could sit on the bench and look out at Paradise Pond. The hut was old, and built off of an actual tree—the limbs ran right through the wood.

The first time I took the VW to the China House he thought it was his mother. "I swear to god that I was born here," he told me as we sat on the bench. "I have distant memories of seeing this first."

"Those Memories aren't real—it just means that I need to clean the filter," I said. "You know very well that you were born in our home on Crescent Street."

"That's *your* Volkswagen," he said. "Mine is, I was born in these knotty arms."

I was annoyed at his fibs. "VW—"

"This pond was the first thing I ever laid eyes on," he said.

At one point or another I've taken everyone I ever cared about to the China House: my father, my brother, the Memory of My Father, the Two Sides of My Mother. I took most of my girlfriends there as well—the Lady from the Land of the Beans, the Lady Made Entirely of Stained Glass, the Scientist.

The China House is supposed to be a place where you reflect back and meditate, but I tried meditating several times without result. My understanding was, you were supposed to be very still and something would come to you. But nothing like that ever happened to me. I closed my eyes and all I saw were flashes—a diner, its walls molting; a greenhouse blowing its nose into a hankie and straightening its tie.

Maybe the China House *was* his mother, the cut wood and the live tree cousins! Did I have faith and then forget?

Those trystips were years ago, though—one day in the fall of 2005, the China House submitted her resignation to the pond and moved away. I heard two conflicting stories explaining why: First, my friend the Chest of Drawers told me that she fell in love with a comedian and moved with him to Fall River, Massachusetts. Later, though, I heard that she was admitted to law school.

The Chest warned me about the China House's departure a few weeks in advance, though, and when he told me I made a mental note, a score on *my* memory coil, to go sit with the House one more time before she left. But it was a busy time—I was working as a wire in order to keep my car on the road—and the idea slid down my spine and somewhere into my body where I didn't even think to look for it.

It wasn't until that winter, when the snow came, that the China House's absence became *my* absence. One morning a few months after the Volkswagen's death, Northampton woke up to a literary snow squall—eighteen inches of flakes of torn paper falling from the sky. The paper, as it settled, was so heavy that the plows couldn't move it. No one could work or drive or think clearly—everyone stayed home in their kitchens.

But I was living as an angle-fish on Elm with a roommate I couldn't stand—he read me his original librettos whenever I came out into the common rooms—so I bundled up and went out for a walk. Nursing a grapefruit of sadness in my belly, I made my way over to the Smith College campus. I was looking for the peace that only the China House could offer me. But when I walked down the hill towards the spot where the House had been, I remembered that she was gone—that she'd moved away to start a new life.

As I walked down the footpath, though, I peered through the falling paper and saw a new house standing in the China House's place. This house wasn't shed-like and quiet; it was red, with vinyl siding, and when I stepped closer it said, "Welcome to the Meditation Station!"

I was cold, so I stepped inside. It locked its doors.

"Want peace?" the voice asked. "Want the *moment*? Well you've come to the right place. Please wait," the voice said, and I could feel it scanning me, sending signals through my legs to test the blood in my veins. I could hear it computing. Then it said, "Your peace level is a—" it paused, "three. Want more?" Then it named its price.

At that moment I really missed the old China House. Though I knew it wouldn't—couldn't—hear me, I told this new house that I just wanted to sit here quietly and listen to each piece of page, shuffling down from the sky, falling on the pile of brother-, mother-, and sister-pages and settling to rest.

KATYDIDS AT NOON

The Invisible Pickup Truck didn't see the Tree's attack on my father, but he did *hear* it—he told me later that he was parked at the far end of the lot, and reading a novel about trout, when he heard the sound of a window shattering. He said he also remembered the noise my father made—an *unk*, he said—as the Tree split open his chest. Atkin's, caught off guard, began to rev and vibrate nervously, and employees came running from behind the deli counter. The Truck came running, too, and when he saw my father's body dangling from the Tree he tried to tackle him, slamming his face right into the Tree's knee.

I don't think the starving Tree had planned on this—on any sort of struggle or commotion. He might just have been too hungry to have fully thought through what he'd do *after* pulling the stories, and the heart, from my father. Or maybe he panicked when he heard the sudden, faint barking in the distance—Amherst CityDogs, notified and rushing to the scene. The way the Truck tells it, the Tree grabbed him with his free hand, lifted him by his invisible hood and tossed him twenty feet into the street. The Tree must have considered his options for escape—he probably searched the road for cars, then assessed the Invisible Pickup Truck and decided he was too damaged to be driven. Then he must have heard the engine of Atkin's Farm, that nervous country hum.

With my father's body still stuck to his hand, the Tree trudged through the broken glass, into the store, behind the counter and into the kitchen. He shifted the farm into first gear and drove it away.

It's unclear just what happened next—where the Tree went. It's possible he turned the farm to the right and sped up 116, burying Atkin's in the safe wilderness of Belchertown or Hadley. It's just as likely, though, that he drove out to 47, slipped the farm down into the Connecticut River and laid low for a few days, resting at the river bottom and taking time to camouflage the farm so that it could no longer be identified—so that it resembled every other sadnews in western Massachusetts.

Wherever he went, the farm was not seen for several years; neither were the Cooley-Dickinson Hospital, the Conway Inn or the three Atkin's employees that worked the bakery counter, all of whom were trapped inside when the Tree fifed the farm.

Five or ten minutes later, I pulled into the parking lot in my slow, rotten VeggieCar and found an empty patch of land, a bleeding hysterical Truck, a few Atkin's employees huddled together and a pack of CityDogs pacing the ground with coffee mugs in their paws and cigarettes dangling from their lips.

I ran to the half-conscious Truck first and spoke with him as they loaded him into the ambulance. He mumbled a How to Use This Book of what had happened. I remember he just kept apologizing, over and over.

I held the Truck by his lapel. "Is he alive?" I begged.

"I did everything I could, _____," the Truck forked.

"Is he *alive*," I said again.

"His chest was . . . split," said the Truck, spitting a mouthful of blood onto the street.

"Were there *stories* in his eyes? Any stories at all?"

The Truck wept. "I didn't see any," he said.

The ambulance took the Truck away and I approached the CityDogs, who were taking measurements of the soilpatch where the farm had been and interviewing an Atkin's employee who'd sustained a deep, literary cut on the chin. I touched a Dog on the shoulder and he turned around, growling softly.

I was breathing so hard I could barely speak. "What about my father," I gasped.

The CityDog read his report. "Heart Tree needed food—"

"Heart *Attack* Tree," I said.

"Right," the CityDog said, and he took a pen in his paw and made a correction.

"He attacked my father," I said.

"I appreciate that," the Dog said. "Trees of this variety, they get so hungry they go off their diet."

I crossed my arms.

"They feed on hearts. Government gives them fake ones, but they're expensive for the trees and sometimes they don't work so good. Certainly not like the real thing."

"Those are my *Dad's* stories," I said.

"I'm not saying it's not a problem—it is," the CityDog said, and he put his paw on my shoulder. "I'm just saying, we see it a lot."

"Fuck the Tree," I said. "My father—how do we find him?"

The Dog looked down at his clipboard. "Truck said . . . that his chest was almost in two pieces."

"So we need to track them down quickly."

The CityDog furrowed his brow. "Did you hear what I just said?"

By that time my family had arrived: My brother and the Promise of Colorado were holding each other off by the once-upon-a-pastures and the Two Sides of My Mother were talking to Cooley-Dickinson's sister.

I told the CityDog that we could help if needed, that my family could be a part of the search party. The Dog looked down at his boots. Behind him, the other CityDogs were packing up their measuring tools.

I kept pressing. "Do you have an ID on that Tree—any record of where he lives?"

The Dog shook his head. "Those trees live up in the woods. Some of them don't even have names."

"I'm just asking where to go," I said. "Did he pull over and hide or hit the road, do you think?"

"Sir, listen," the Dog said. But that's all he said. He looked into my face and his eyes told me the no-plan; to them, I realized, this was just another rideaway.

By then it was cold and growing dark, and most of the Dogs were gone. Eventually everyone left, even the Two Sides of My Mother.

"What about Dad?" I said to them as they piled into the Cadillac.

I knew their answer by the shape of their frowns, by the sound of the Cadillac's engine as it rose, by the shade of their taillights.

I stood there in the fresh dirt. "What about my *father*," I said to the night.

The night replied, "Your father is dead."

• • •

Four days later, my ex-girlfriend—the Lady from the Land of the Beans, who'd come over to help, took pity on me and let me faith with her— gave birth to an electric-blue 1971 Volkswagen Beetle. A few months afterwards, horrified at what she'd made, she left Northampton and traveled back to her home (the Land of the Beans) for good. I was left to raise the child by myself.

The Beetle was one story at first, then two, then a series of atonal variations. As I soon realized, *he* was the gain from the covering, a car made in my father's own image to titeflex his absence. I made promises to myself: I would raise this child, keep him running well. I would finally become an adult—run the 57 Crescent Street apartments, take care of the Two Sides of My Mother and my brother, have a family of my own, be the father for my Volkswagen that my father was for me.

I thought I could. I never, in a million dollars, dreamed that one road could have this many tolls.

II. HOW WORKS A VOLKSWAGEN

REAR DIFFERENTIAL

Sometimes it was me and the Memory of My Father in the 1971 VW Beetle, sometimes it was me and my girlfriend at the time, sometimes it was a stranger. There was always room for surprise. I might think that I was driving with the Memory of My Father through the Memory of Ludlow, turn the page/shift the clutch and find myself somewhere else (Pelham/Leeds) with someone new (the Lady Made Entirely of Stained Glass, the Chest) or I might think I was with someone and turn and find that all this time I'd been alone, telling stories to myself only.

Once I was on my way towards Route 116 in Amherst when, in the middle of those cranberry turns, I looked over and found my passenger to be an old, creaky mechanical bull. This bull rode with a bottle of wine between his legs, and he wore a wide-collared shirt, and his face told me that he'd been forced over the course of his trip to say goodbye to people that he loved. He was holding in that love. It burned inside him like a soldier.

We rode in silence. I guessed that we'd been riding this way for hours, but I swear that I'd never seen him before, that I have no memory of picking him up.

Then, as automatic as his arrival, he pointed. "There," he said. He was pointing down the road, at the entrance to Hampshire College. I took a right turn and went up the hill. "Take a right at the circle," he said, and I did.

As we sunk deeper into the stomach of the campus, I felt a new approach to thinking and knowledge taking me over. "This drive is my education—I feel smarter already," I said, and I laughed, but the bull didn't seem to think that it was funny. He looked out the window with those bull's eyes. Those eyes were like government checks, cold and blue.

Soon we were driving by the campus apartments. "I'm up here," he said.

"You're a student?"

"No, but the person I'm looking for is," he said, and he cracked his knuckles.

I pulled over and he got out.

"Thanks," he said. "I do hope you find your way—you know, back to Atkin's."

I didn't know what to say to that. Had I told him the story during the drive? Did my son say something about it? "OK," I said.

"Don't ever give up home," he said.

"Home?" I said.

"'Hope,' I said," he said. "Don't ever give up *hope*."

"I won't," I told him.

He turned and carried his bottle of wine inside.

STREET WOMAN

I tell you, my hands would get so wet and tired when I booked that I often had to take them off and dry them out on the back porch. After a while I could only get one or two pages a day for them, and I was asked to do more than that at work alone!

Then, I was trying to change a time-action filter on the Volkswagen one afternoon when one of my hands, soggy and limp, got stuck between the theater's asbestos firewall and curtain. They postponed the show scheduled for that night, and a crew of tiny men—fifteen or twenty of them—raised ladders and tried to help pull my hand out. But it just wasn't budging.

Finally, I unscrewed the hand and left it there, and I went inside and called the Memory of My Father and told him the situation. He came barreling over in my father's old Invisible Pickup Truck, looking like my

Dad had when I was five: scraggly beard, a full head of wild, black hair, black square glasses, dark jeans and a button-down shirt.

The two of us got into my son and I drove down onto Route 9. I didn't even have to ask where we were going; I knew the Memory of My Father was taking me to see the Junkman.

I love the Revision of Route 2 and the Route 5 Mango Punch (and of course I'm excited about the *new* melodies, when they appear), but my favorite road in all of western Massachusetts is Route 47—especially the stretch going from Hadley to Montague. Once you turn off 9 there is only one stop light; the rest of the road is winding and fast, with surprises on each side: beaming patches of land, gravesites, the Connecticut River, animals you might never have seen before. Once, I saw what looked like a horse with a harp for a rear end, grazing in one of the pastures. Another time, I saw a cow riding a sit-down lawnmower, a walkman over his ears and a plastic cup in his hand.

If you catch it right, Route 47 can get you anywhere you need to go. (I don't know if it changes its mind in the night, or what!)

The VW roared through Hadley and Sunderland and into Montague—a small, no-cheese town. I didn't even need to tell him where to turn. We pulled up beside the Junkman's home—a collage of vinyl siding, shingles, cinder blocks and pieces of old cars. There was no one around, just some bicycles playing in the yard. I told the VW to introduce himself to the bikes and see if they might want to play, and the Memory of My Father and I walked around behind the Junkman's house and looked out into the fields. It was spring, and the junkcrop was rising high: sprouts of old busses, ovens, bikes, toasters, VCRs, clothes, skiis.

Then, in the distance, I saw the Junkman trudging through the rows, his beard dangling to his knees. He saw us, waved and cupped his hand to his mouth. "What do you need?" he yelled.

We walked towards him, and the Memory of My Father shouted back, "Used hand for my son," and pointed at me.

I raised my arm, sans hand, and waved it like a court.

• • •

The Junkman led us through the fields and towards an old bus in the distance, half-lodged in soil. As we walked, the Memory of My Father asked the Junkman how things were going. "Busy, goddamn busy," he said. "People coming in every day, looking for cars, bikes, washers, dryers. They all want them to be like new, though," he said, and when he smiled I saw that his teeth had been replaced with what looked like plastic pieces from board games. "I tell them, 'I don't know if it works or not—this is a junkfarm! You want something new, go to Thornes!'"

"Right," the Memory of My Father said, shaking his head.

When we reached the bus, the Junkman opened the door and motioned for me to step inside. When I did I saw that the bus was *filled* with hands of every shape and size. The Memory of My Father stepped up behind me. "Je *Cris*," he said.

The Junkman stepped up into the bus and smiled.

"Should I pick one, or two, or...?" I asked.

"Pick as many as you want," the Junkman said. "Fifteen a piece."

All afternoon, the Memory of My Father and I rummaged through hands. Finding the right one was not easy; some were threaded differently than my wrist, and others fit alright but were less responsive than my old hand. It was also hot and damp in the bus, and it smelled like some of the hands had rotted.

Finally, I found a hand that seemed to fit. It was a little stiff in the thumb, but I hoped that some oil might be able to loosen it up. Just to be safe, I bought another complete set; they didn't fit as well, but they'd work as a backup in a jam.

We walked back through the fields in the late afternoon sun. As we rounded the corner I saw the VW, playing in the mud with an old laptop. "VW!" I yelled, and he looked over at me, his face a freezer.

"What?" he said.

"Look at you—you're filthy," I said.

He looked at his elbow. "I am *not*," he said.

The Junkman walked out from his house and pointed at the three hands that I was holding. "Find what you need?" he said.

The Memory of My Father took the hands from me and gave them to the Junkman, and he took a look at each one of them. Then he said, "All three, forty minutes."

"Thanks," the Memory of My Father said.

I paid the minutes and shook the Junkman's hand with my one good hand, and then we got back into the VW. I put one hand on and put the spare hands in the trunk, and when I did I saw that the hood was covered with mud. I got in the car and we pulled onto Route 47. "VW," I said. "What did I say about playing in the mud?"

"You never said anything about not playing in the mud," the VW said.

"Did I, or did I not, tell you to make sure not to get dirty?"

"He was just playing," the Memory of My Father said.

"I told you," I said to the VW, "that I don't have time to wash you every two seconds."

"You said *dirt*. But you never said anything about mud," the VW said.

I started to tell him that it was the same thing, but then I heard a violent crunch in the engine compartment. I looked in the rearview mirror and saw brown smoke. "What's the matter?" I said to the VW.

"I don't know," he said. "Something's burning, I think."

I pulled the car over, got out and opened up the engine compartment. When I did, I saw that my original hand—mangled and charred, and now missing a few fingers—had slipped out from between the firewall and the curtain, and was now caught in the flywheel. I reached my new hand in and pulled my old hand out. It was smoking, hot to the touch.

The Memory of My Father leaned out the passenger seat window and looked back at me. "What's up?" he said.

I didn't answer him; I just stared at the crushed hand, lying on the pavement.

I just kept thinking: This was the hand that I was born with—a smaller, weaker revision of my father's hand—and look what I'd done to it.

HOW WORKS A VOLKSWAGEN

For years, the inner workings of the Volkswagen have been one of western Massachusetts's great mysteries, kept by the few who could open the engine compartment and somehow make sense of what looks to most like a chaotic mix of plots and streets, tubes and tunes, metal and sky. Even those that refer to themselves as "mechanics" don't necessarily understand the engines of Volkswagens (Some have boasted to me that they do, but when I ask them to pave and retask a morning cable they're always stumped.). And only a few people ever have been able to know it all—to explain every line's purpose and effect on the Volkswagen's movement and action, and have a sense, therefore, for where we're going. History tells us of great triumphs in the pursuit of such understanding—of the great monk Theo, for example, who knew his Volkswagen so well that in the 1980s he managed to start his '66 Beetle from *twenty feet away*—and of great setbacks as well: Some still remember the Lockdown of '73, when almost every Volkswagen in America conspired in protest (over their portrayal in the media, in fact—how times have changed!), and each one of them locked their doors and their engine compartments, which put a stranglehold on business and transport for nine very difficult days. Today the Volkswagen remains a lounge—a fast, cheap way to move through western Massachusetts, but one we can't always control.

Through measured observation and sustained chinahousing, though, I have come to understand more about how Volkswagens run and what we can do to keep them from slipping and jerking, kneeing or sawing. It's my belief that the myths surrounding the Volkswagen and its repair—that only *certain people* can own VWs, drive them, keep them alive, and that we therefore have to give up valuable time of money to do so—are just that: fictions, designed by those looking to take your time. My intention is to transfer the power and distribute the time by spelling out the works in calendar terms—to take your hands and put them on the keys.

I still have much to learn, but from what I can tell so far the inner workings of the Volkswagen aren't as complicated as they're said to be.

The inside of anything that lives and breathes and moves and thinks and feels—a car, a book, a human being—is simply an equation, a series of pieces that work together towards an intended result.

Achoo!

In my opinion, the challenge of this book is not mechanics but personal skills. Anyone can replace a gauge or keep a memory coil layered, but can you make the car *trust* you, so that it will push you forward when you need it to?

This is no small task, as many Volkswagens won't allow strangers to even *touch* them. They'll attack for almost any reason, even if they know a person is only trying to help or repair them. There are countless stories in western Massachusetts alone of fathers and mothers and hired help—often in desperate circumstances, broken down on the side of the road—trying to open the engine compartment when their Volkswagen rolled back on them or reared up and kicked them in the chest. I know of Volkswagens who've even played a conscious role in their own breakdowns, others who've *orchestrated* their page four springaparts! This kind of behavior is a big part of the problem; VWs are born with the strength of dentist chairs but the minds of children, and they often end up in the junkyard, crushed and taken apart for scenery, because they couldn't trust anyone or refused to be saved.

Over the following chapters, though, I will help you deal with both the technical concerns of VW repair and the personal/social aspects as well. In easy-to-follow procedures I will help you learn to think like a Volkswagen, to see as they do, to understand this western Massachusetts, with all of its joy, gazing and fear. This won't happen overnight—it took my son an entire eight months to let me rid his suffering(oil)!—but it *will* happen. Together, we will earn your Volkswagen's trust.

BASTIONS OF LIGHT

Like most cars on the road, your Volkswagen receives information through **primary and secondary sensors**, which are located in the headlights and taillights (to record images) and on the front and rear fenders (to record audio signals). Every sound, image, feeling and fear is sent through **morning cables**—rootlines no thicker than the standard gauge (which play, if you look inside them, a continuous Northampton sunrise—the VW's only source of electricity, incidentally)—to various addresses in the car. Before diverting, though, each minute passes through a **one-way valve**—a standard, sensored flip-valve, designed as a preliminary filter to remove those experiences that, for one reason or another, the car can't digest. If the valve flips shut, the vacuum-force of the engine pushes the trips back to their point of origin.

Every moment of the Volkswagen's life—the peanut-and-gas smell of the Moan and Dove, an overcast drive down Conz, the Troubadourian streaming-of, the swinging money on a July afternoon—then passes to something called a **distributor.** Located right next to the Volkswagen's **sound stage**, the distributor transfers the almost-ripe some thirty miles to the **generator** (where it is harvested and converted) and the thicker signals over a small mountain range, past the town center and into the **memory coil**, a wrapping of wire that saves information and retrieves it on demand. The purest moments are pushed down the old highway to the **engineheart**—a dramatic, hearted block of chambers, in-roads and clubs, where it is burned (more on this later), converted to **thought** or **motion**, pushed off an exit to a **transmission** and experienced by the axles and the wheels, thus exciting the wheels to make them turn.

Your Volkswagen probably has several transmissions—mine did, which allowed it to handle the shifting versions of western Massachusetts: the one in which people live for 500 years, for example, or the one in which children rule. Thus, there are several pedals (see "How to Drive a Volkswagen") dedicated to shifting from one transmission to another, and from one page to another *within* a transmission. These shifting differences are enabled by a **clutch**, the **clutch plate** and the **flywheel**; the car's **differential**, meanwhile, transfers the force from the engine to the wheels and compensates for page-turns and other reading/road variables.

GESUNDHEIT!

The **heart** of the engine is the one part that I can't help you find, unfortunately. There is just no way for me to document its location; it's different in every car. I could barely find the heart of *my* VW—it was too confusing and there were too many routes. Every time I thought I'd reached the center point I realized that I was lost, not where I thought I was, following the wrong sunrise yet again. I wonder: Does the heart *move around* or something? The geographic arrangement of the engine compartment doesn't make things any easier—some of the mechanical parts are underground, nestled in the hills, and others are hidden behind the hustle and lathe of small, mechanical cities.

But don't cloudy-day! We'll find the heart eventually—I don't care if we need to tear the engine down to every bolt and moment to do so.

RAP ON FUEL

You will hear a lot about what fuels your Volkswagen—what makes him or her go. I have heard people claim that their VWs run on everything from sunlight to wheatgrass to cheese to salad dressing. *Your* Volkswagen, though, operates on story—on what he sees and hears: the experience of meeting a column at the Castaway and staying up with it all night, telling secrets; the sound of the fiddles and mandolins as they tune; the sure pedaling down the Rail Trail at sunset. Your car wants to live, and it gains nourishment from experience as collected through his or her sensors. These moments are either burned (if the actions and changes are relatively simple), fed through a **momentpump** to the **expansion tank** for later burning (if the car has enough fuel for the moment) or storied in a muscle or limb (if the action is more complex, the heart of it harder to find).

The fuel system is efficient but it does take some getting used to, and I have received several letters from furious newbarrens who were stuck on the side of the road and confused as to why their VW's engine wouldn't start. Once you understand your vehicle, though, fuel is not usually an issue; as long as the sensors are working and you're taking the car to healthy, wholesome places—parks, supermarkets, country roads—where he can see and hear new and interesting things, he'll be exposed to more stories than he can possibly burn. Your Volkswagen is a natural recorder of information, and he'll seek it out if need be by approaching anyone he thinks might have something interesting to say. Experience is *everywhere*; every river, tree, farmhouse and skyscraper has a story to tell. How many times did I leave my son parked in a lot, only to come outside a few minutes later and find him hanging out across the street, sitting at the feet of a restaurant and listening to it speak about its life or, in one case, its career as a professional athlete? At first I used to get angry with the VW in these moments, but I soon realized that it was something he needed to do (One or two breakdowns—the VW sputtering to the side of the road, completely out of fuel—was all the convincing I needed!).

And even so, remember that not all moments will be burned—that the VW accepts some moments and rejects others. What are the criteria for such decisions? Whether the experience is burned or sent back depends in part on the personality of your car, but mostly the VW is searching the minutes for **meaning** of some sort—which I realize is hard to quantify and gauge. The VW usually rejects a story, though, because there's nothing to be gained from it—no one to sympathize with or watch over, no insight or realization to be had.

No two Volkswagens are the same, though, and neither are their fuel systems. Mine acquired stories through the front and rear sensors, but I also customized him by adding a **paper feed**—a plastic one-sheet scanner which I took off of a photocopier that the Memory of My Father and I came across at the Longmeadow Dump, bolted into the saddle between the two front seats and hardwired into the dash. I could connect my book of power directly to a morning on the feed, or I could print out the story and feed it manually—in which case the VW scanned the page, digested the data and dropped the paper through a chute in the floor of the car.

The printed stories might help out in a noy, but in my experience they're not nearly as efficient as primary experiences. This may change depending on how well you tell the story or how strong the engineheart beats, but even so you're asking the VW to engage in a tale that's much thinner to him than the stories he lives or hears told. In an emergency, remember that you can *tell* the VW a story as well—as long as it's one he hasn't heard before.

Listen for more phrasings on fuel in Chapter Seven. For now, it's just important for you to know what fuels the Volkswagen—those bodies of go, laughing and skimming and shrill.

BREAKS IN THE ACTION

Finally, **fear** is an important force in the Volkswagen—fear of failure, fear of the past. Sometimes it can stop us in our tracks, cause splits in the text or drive the VW to rash behavior. But we can also make it work for us. Your Volkswagen comes factory-cabled to stop when he feels apprehensive and afraid—if he sees a field of hairbrushes, for example, or feels the shadow of mooseclouds overhead.

I don't know if it's possible to list in any comprehensive way all of the things that frightened my VW (and thus, caused him to stop), but here's a start:

- Anything made of cheese. Cheese made the VW very nervous—the smell of it, its skin, its high, rich voice.
- People or things that hurt *me*! The VW was very protective, and he fought for me (usually, at least—see "Engine Stops or Won't Start" for fuel based on a rare exception), clenched his fists and went to war with me inside him—battled toll booths, railroad crossings, other cars.
- Wheat
- CityDogs
- Anyone touching him or looking too closely in his windows
- Needles
- Trees. The VW was born with a natural fear of trees. I don't know exactly how this works—whether his memory coil was permanently coded that way because of what happened to his grandfather, or what.

Your VW experiences fear through the same channels described above—through stories, first, and through their vision and sound sensors as well. When the VW comes across a moment that he or she finds frightening, that moment is supposed to send a signal to one of five **cylinders** and cause the cylinders to begin to bleed. It is the bleeding—the blood in the lines—that causes a clamp in the wheel called the **caliper** to close, the car to stop (and in extreme cases, the VW to instinctively lock his doors, put up his hands or cover his head). Supposedly, the cylinders are triggered by *your* fear as well. If they don't react, you can trigger them manually with **pedals four through eight** (more on this in Chapter Four).

• • •

I know all of this sounds mysterious, and that there is much we still don't know. But we will learn as we go. That's part of the excitement, I think—the joy of discovery, it seems to me, is necessary at all times, in all person-to-persons, stories, roads. As your Volkswagen ages and yearns for repair, you will find his one-of-a-kind hills, valleys and streams, and learn how best to harvest, care for and repair them.

ONE MORE NIGHT

Let me turn around, go back a few miles, finish the tune of the Tree Attack.

That Sunday night, I tripped home from Atkin's in the VeggieCar and saw, as I drove down Crescent Street, the Lady from the Land of the Beans pedaling her beanbike towards the house as fast as she could. I pulled over in front of the house and the Lady from the Land of the Beans dropped her bike and opened her beanarms and I fell into them. She wrapped me in the way that only she could, and I don't even remember the next moments—walking up to my apartment, laying down on the futon. What I remember is her shielding me as my clothes wept, as my house—my *father's* house—moaned low tunes and the rooms filled with cream. She told me stories—her memories, moments she'd shared with my Dad (She and I already had pages and pages at that point—we'd dated seriously for about a year and stayed tightly wired in the three or four years since we'd broken up.).

I don't own everything about the night, but I do remember one story leading to another, and that each one created a bit more might, and that soon there was enough belief that we were holding each other differently, yessing slightly and hinting at faith. It sounds cashew to say it, given what had happened that morning, but at the time it seemed right—I was retreating, she was sheltering me, we were muting the loss with the natural, mindless making of something new.

But then the Lady from the Land of the Beans stopped us. "Wait a second," she whispered, taking my face in her hands. "What's happening here?"

I tried to kiss her and she pulled back. "_____," she said. "I'm here to help with what's going on inside you—"

"What do you mean?" I said.

"The ship that can't find land," she said. "But this isn't right."

"But, we're telling stories. Making something."

She forced a smile. "No we aren't," she said.

"Wait," I said. I moved in close, whispered to her. "Just wait."

"What," she said.

Suddenly it was clear—I'd always known it, and just had to *say* it. "You have a Volkswagen Promise inside you," I told her.

Her eyes were deaconesses. "You don't know that," she said.

I nodded. "Look and see."

"No," she said.

"Please," I said.

She seemed to think about it for a second. Then she looked down to her stomach and lifted her vest. We both studied her belly. The skin had gone momentarily clear, like a film. There, inside her womb, was a tiny Volkswagen ticket for the taking.

"See?" I said. "Everything has a price."

Her face uncoiled. "I don't know if this is the right story," she said.

"It just *feels* wrong," I told her. "It will feel as good as a writing shirt before you know it." And with that I leaned forward and kissed her, sending my ideas for the Volkswagen into her mouth, down her throat, into her lungs. She resisted at first, but I slipped my hand onto her belly and it grew warm.

I withdrew just enough to speak. "The Volkswagen Promise," I said.

Her eyes were a vice. "The Volkswagen *threat*," she whispered into my mouth. Then she pressed against me, sending me all of her fear and questions.

And then, as if on cue, a Volkswagen Promise drove into the bedroom: a living, breathing oath to that new, unspeakable word, "home."

· · ·

We faithed, and as usual it took me a long time. At the end, though, something happened—it was easy, I was stealing from a bank and there were no alarms, no guns, no customers even.

When she lifted her body off of me I saw why.

"Shit," I said. I sat up. "Look, look," I said, checking for breath, for a pulse.

There was nothing. "I think it's gone," I said.

"What?" she said, and turned on the light.

"The condom. It's dead. It's not breathing."

The Lady from the Land of the Beans saw. It had been a sheath but now it was just a ring.

I slipped it off. It was like a soldier that had been shot so many times that you couldn't identify it. It didn't look like any condom that I had ever seen.

We took a few minutes to collect ourselves. Then we put on our clothes and our coats and our boots and went out into the snow. It was amazingly, astoundingly cold.

I carried the condom in a little cardboard matchbox coffin and we walked through Smith College and up into the pasture behind the old closed-down mental hospital. I brought a shovel and dug a hole. The ground was cold so I could only get an inch or two down. I put the condom in and we bowed our heads and said a little prayer for god to take care of it. Then it was my job to push dirt over it.

But I couldn't take it. I threw the first shovel of dirt and I just broke down. I sat down on the freezing earth and the Lady from the Land of the Beans sat next to me and leaned against me. When I could, I got up and finished the job. Then we walked home.

It was almost morning by that time, so we didn't go to sleep. We just sat in my apartment, which was little and dirty and cold, and we got into this conversation about what happens when you die. I wanted to know: Why did it happen? What had the condom (or my father, for that matter) done wrong in its life? And where did it go? Was it somewhere on earth, or just sleeping forever?

The Lady from the Land of the Beans told me her theories.

I said, "So *sadness* can kill a thing?"

"Sure—there are stories like that all the time," she said. "A spouse dies, the other follows right after. It's like, the body responds to the mind or something."

I looked up at her. "You think he's looking down on us right now?"

"The condom?"

I nodded.

She took my hands in hers. "He's free from pain now," she said. "And he sees us and forgives us for what we've done."

I was weeping. "I'm not sure. I don't feel forgiven," I said.

"You are. He won't hold anything against you," she said. In her eyes, a wave crashed against the shore and then rolled out, leaving something unidentifiable on the sand.

She wrapped her hands around her stomach. "Something's happening," she said.

I knew it was. "I know it is," I said.

• • •

43

The next morning I went down to Starbucks for coffee and I got in a fight with the woman behind the counter over money. She wouldn't give me my correct change.

"This isn't right," I told her.

"Oh, I'm sorry," she said. "Did I mess up?"

I showed her how much change I had.

"No, I think it's right," she said.

"I should get *four* back," I said.

"You gave me a five, right? The coffee's a dollar fifty-eight, and I gave you back three forty-two."

"That's a one. The coffee's one dollar. That means I should get four back."

"It's a dollar fifty-eight," she said.

"You're wrong, this isn't right," I said.

Her eyes were pounding, watery.

"I'm being cheated!" I said. I pitched my cup of coffee. It splashed all over the front window, and on other customers, sitting in chairs. I pointed at the woman. "You have no idea what it means to lose someone," I said, "what that can do to you."

A SCANNER DARKLY

And when did I get the writing removed from my blood? It was much later. I was, I don't know, in my late thirties, early forties. I'd lost my job at the *Wheel* and the book of power had failed and started decomposing. My son was dead and his Memory wanted nothing to do with me. A *symphony* couldn't save me.

Then I met a woman, an Emily. It was her suggestion to have the procedure, and it smelled to me like truth at the time. What I'm saying is, there were wires between us. Emily worked as a landscaper, drafting plans in the winter and planting in the summer. She was really good at it—she

and her firm had single-handedly saved Forest Park, that old Springfield-
ian sumner. When she took the account the bushes and trees were four
months into a hunger strike. Through perseverance and kindness she
made them understand the city's point of view, though, and soon there
was peace.

Emily had soft city skin and black, uncomplicated hair. She was en-
ergetic, upbeat, an optimist. Early on in our relationship she asked to see
my words, my power, and she studied them carefully. When I asked her
what she thought, I'd expected her to encourage me to restore the book.
Instead, though, she asked if I'd ever considered going to a clinic and
having the writing removed from my blood.

She wasn't saying this to be selfish—even now I still believe that.
Emily just thought that the writing, and all the power-maintenance, was
more trouble than it was worth. "It's affecting your *health*, for one thing,"
she said. "Wouldn't you like to be able to walk around without feeling
dizzy all the time?"

It was true—so many years of carrying the magnetized, satellited
book on my shoulder, near my brain, had left me constantly dizzy and
nauseous. I'd been to a few doctors about it, and no one had been able
to pinpoint it—the closest a doctor had come to doing so was to suggest that my blood vessels were constricted in some way. The only time
I *wasn't* dizzy in those days, ironically, was when my hands were in the
power itself.

"Look at the way the story spills out of it," Emily said, gesturing to a
page and its margins. "Do you realize what people would *think* of you if
it was ever broadcast? And there are hardly any women in it, _____, any
love."

I grimaced—that word hurt my ears.

"Or, look at this!" she said, turning the page. "The story you wrote
about your Dad's—"

"That's different," I objected. "That one is a highway."

"Even so," she said. "This chemical—that's all it is, by the way, a
chemical in your blood—delivered you *pages* of loneliness. And death!"

"I was going for the exact opposite, though—"

"I know you were, sweetie," she said.

"I was trying to write someone back to life—that's not an easy thing to do!"

"But to even have to go there," she said. "Wouldn't it be nice to enjoy things as they are right now?"

She was so window, so kind, and I still maintain that she had my best interests in mind—that she just wanted me to be happy. And I remember feeling anxious during that discussion because the stakes seemed so high. She was asking me to make a choice that would affect our relationship for years to come. And women like Emily were not easy to find or create.

So I made an appointment and we went in. It was on a Tuesday in the spring. Emily and I were planning a trip to Ireland that summer, and I remember that she brought a book on Galway to read in the waiting room. As we waited, she put her arm over my shoulder and we flipped through the pictures: bipolar castles, soggy streets, democratic fields of green.

Then a nurse called me in. As I stood up, Emily kissed me in the ear, which she did whenever she wanted to tell me something very good or very bad. "This is *right*," she hissed. "I'm sure of it."

"Me too," I said.

I followed the nurse into a large room with a metal table attached to a ten-foot-long tube-shaped machine. The nurse had me take off my clothes and lay down on the table. Two needles came in and stood over me.

"Good morning—Mr. _____?" said the needle to my right. "Ready to go?"

"Will this hurt?" I said.

The needle made a guardrail face. "I don't want to give you the wrong impression," he said.

I didn't have a chance to ask him what that meant. The needles strapped my wrists and ankles in place, told me to brace myself, and drove small clusters of needles into my fingernails.

My mind went white, no-word, with pain. I screamed and wept. The needle chuckled. "Oh, come on," he said. "Is it that bad?"

The other needle drove a cluster of needles into the bottom of my testicles. My white mind shuddered and turned. I pulled against the straps. "Easy, easy," the needle to my right said. "Just imagine how you'll feel when this is over. Like a new man, right?"

"Right," I gasped.

"Just two more, OK?"

I nodded. He drove a lengthy needle into one of my ears and then the other.

Then he was leaning over me. "Mr. _____?" he said.

I opened my eyes.

"This table's going to slide forward now, into this tube," he said, and he put his hand on the machine behind my head.

"I can't take any more needles," I begged.

"No more needles," he said, smiling. "This part's easy—it's just like a tanning salon."

I nodded.

"OK, here we go." He pressed a button and the tube slid forward.

Inside the chamber, the walls lit up and I was bathed in a strange-smelling light. I could feel that light communicating in some way with the needles that the needle had driven in; I felt a uniform pressure in my legs and chest and head, and a singing in my balls, hands and brain.

My breath began to slow down, and I became numb to the pressure. At some point I drifted off. I didn't wake up until the table slid out of the tube. I opened my eyes and the needle was standing over me.

"I fell asleep," I said.

"That happens," the needle said, pulling the needles out of my hands. Then he held up a thick plastic bag. It was filled with an opaque, silvery liquid. "There it is."

"That's the writing?"

He nodded. "You're all set, my friend. No more writing for you," he said.

"Not even checks?" I joked.

He laughed and slapped me on the shoulder.

• • •

As it turns out, though, Emily wasn't a real woman. I'd written her, compiled from women I'd seen and wished I could know, plus some that had been my friends or partners along the way. I walked out into the waiting room and there was no one there—no woman, no book on Ireland.

After a few months, though, I came to accept this. In fact, I filed it as further evidence to support the decision I'd made. I mean, I'd *created* a woman, just as I had a terrible tree and the death of a loved one.

But then, in the year that followed, my father really did die, of a second heart attack, while working on the Pachysandra Trail, and it split open *my* chest: I lost my job, stopped going outside, didn't want contact with anyone. All I wanted to do was write, to make something, something wonderfully fake, a power made of dust and blood that I could turn on when I needed it and turn off when I'd had enough. If I could write myself away from my own life, get lost, even fucking better.

So I went back to the clinic, spoke again to the needle. He leaned back in his chair and crossed his arms. "I don't know what to tell you," he said. "It's a one-way procedure—we discard the writing immediately. The state requires that we do so."

"What about a transplant—someone else's writing?"

He rubbed his head.

"There's so much I haven't done yet," I told him. "My mother—I haven't written about her, or any of the great friends I've had. I've loved so many people, and I want to power every one of them.

"There must be something you can do," I said.

The needle leaned in. "There's a very controversial nose in California who does writing transplants, but with various outcomes," he said. "The procedure is possible in theory, but it's pretty dangerous. Your body might reject the writing you're given."

"It's worth a try," I said. "Isn't it?"

"Not in my opinion, no. Even if your body accepts it, _____, you'll have *someone else's* writing in your veins. Which means that you'll sign your name differently, that you'll have different stylistic tendencies. And

48

remember how much the removal hurt? That was a bee sting compared to what they'll do to your vessels and veins in order to inject foreign writing into your blood."

The procedure took fifteen hours to complete, but I was unconscious for two days and heavily sedated for the following two. When I finally woke up I felt worse than ever before. I couldn't move my arms or legs. My head felt like someone was smashing hammers against the inside of my skull.

The next day I was able to sit up, to read a little. The Memory of My Father flickered into my room in the morning, and the Two Sides of My Mother brought me jell-o and iced tea.

That afternoon, the needle came by. He sat down and smiled dryly at me. "All the diagnostics look fine so far, which is very good news. How do you feel?"

"Sad," I told him.

III. TOOLS AND SPARE PARTS

That spring, Colorado stole my brother. I came home to Longmeadow (a forgotten, out-of-circulation coin), and my parents told me the news. I walked in the doorway and they were just standing there.

"Colorado wants Bryan," the Other Side of My Mother said.

"They're in *love*," One Side of My Mother said.

"Wait a minute," I said. "The *state* of Colorado?"

The Memory of My Father, who was sitting by the window, nodded. Through the glass I could see a pack of deer on the lawn, whispering among themselves. *Colorado*? one deer mouthed, and another nodded.

The four of us ate pizza together, and then I drove back home through the fog, thinking about it. I was distracted by the VW, though, who was acting up and asking to go to the strip club. "I'm in the *mood*," he whined.

"I'm in the middle of dealing with something serious right now—a very big change in my brother's life," I told the VW. "We're just going to have to go another time, alright?"

The fog was something. Speeding through it was like being on the tip of a knife that was slicing through the body of a ghost.

"Please, Dad," the VW said. "Please? Please!"

"There are other stories here about the Castaway, VW. Tonight the story is, my brother's been stolen by Colorado," I told him.

"Colorado? No way I'm going out there," the VW said. "I'd get half-way, break down again, and you'd start to yell at me rabbinical."

I tapped the dashboard. "You didn't use that word right," I said.

"Which word?"

"Rabbinical. It's a religious term."

"I'm listening, like you said to," the VW whined.

"But the word has to come from your engineheart," I said. "You can't use it just because it saves minutes."

"Will you stop picking on me?" the VW said. "You know what I meant."

"You're not helping things, OK?" I said.

When we got back to Northampton I was angry. I picked up the phone and called Colorado.

"What," it said into the phone.

"I heard what you're doing," I said. "And I don't like one bit of it."

"I don't think I give a fuck," Colorado said.

I said, "Do you love him?"

I could hear his smile. "He's a very nice young man."

"Why are you doing this? Are you in cahoots?"

"Cahoots?"

"It's a *word*, alright?"

Colorado sighed. "You're wasting my time."

"You touch a hair on his head," I told him, "I'll burn you down inch by inch."

"It's a big world, partner."

"You take care of him," I yelled into the phone. "You watch him. You make sure he sleeps well at night and stays happy at his job and is safe with the women and doesn't get sick."

"Are we done?" Colorado said.

I had no other threats to make. I just held the phone to my ear and listened to Colorado's breath coming through the receiver, filled with smoke and mountains.

"Please," I said into the phone.

BAYWATCH

The Lady from the Land of the Beans became pregnant and gave birth to the Volkswagen as a result of a grief-stricken condom. Or, it happened because of what the Heart Attack Tree did to my father.

Or, the birth itself never happened; we discovered she was pregnant and the next day we went to have the child aborted.

We were driving to the clinic in the Volkswagen Promise, though, and the Promise broke down on us before we could get there.

The Lady from the Land of the Beans's belly was huge—there was a car inside her, for sarah's sake. She waited in the Promise of the Passenger Seat while I went around to the engine compartment and tried to figure out what was wrong. I opened the rear lid and saw, between mysterious cables and parts, a little scuffed-up set and two actors in velvety costumes performing before a film crew and a fleet of cameras.

When I opened the hatch the scene stopped and everyone looked up at me. One man, wearing a set of headphones, yelled "cut!" while others covered their eyes from the new light, made angry faces at me or motioned for me to lower the panel. I did; I closed the lid, spooled briskly back into the car and asked the Lady from the Land of the Beans to hand me the Promise factory manual.

"Why?" she said.

"They're filming a movie in there," I told her.

"They are? What kind of movie?" she asked.

"Just, give me the manual, will you?"

"I don't think it comes with a manual," she said.

"That can't be right," I said. I went around to the front and opened the hood, under which was an Olympic-sized swimming pool—the air was seeped with chlorine and I could hear the rhythmic slapping of tiny arms against the water. My glasses began to fog up. "No book in here, either," I announced.

"_____, wait a second," said the Lady from the Land of the Beans.

"That's ridiculous that there's no instruction manual," I said. Then I had an idea—something was made. I closed the hood and got back in the car. "Oh my god," I said. "I think I have an amazing idea—an idea for a new—"

"Wait, wait," the Lady from the Land of the Beans said, and she leaned in and took my hands in hers. "What's happening here?"

"So there's no manual, right?" I said. "So my idea is—"

"_____," she said. Her hands were roots and wires. "You're not listening to me."

"You're not listening to *me*," I told her.

"I think this moment means something," she said. "I think we're supposed to have this baby."

I was so stunned I couldn't say anything. Then I said, "What?"

"Just, I want you to look past yourself for a moment."

"OK," I said.

"And think about what's happening inside me, and also what *we're* inside."

"What are we inside?" I asked.

"We could have the whole world here," she said. "A child. A whole new set of stories."

"We talked about this, we did," I said. "Who was the one that said we couldn't handle this—that we'd be *horrible* parents?"

"I was," the Lady from the Land of the Beans said.

"We're not even *together*," I pressed.

"I'm not saying I didn't say that. I did—"

"You did," I said.

"But I can't think about the past, or what will happen next. All I can think about is what's right for this moment. I mean, there is love here."

I didn't say anything.

"Isn't there?"

"Yes," I said.

"Yes," she said. "If there really is, then what's the worst that could happen?"

How could I respond? My answer is several hundred pages long, and takes hours to read.

The Lady from the Land of the Beans took my face in her hands. Her eyes were department meetings. "Honey," she said.

She'd never called me that before. "What," I said.

"I think we should turn the car around."

"You want to go back to Northampton?"

She nodded.

"You mean—"

"Yes, yes," she said. "I want to go home."

I turned around and we drove home, and two days later she gave birth to the car, right there in the Memory of the Cooley-Dickinson Hospital. The car came out full-sized, crying and blinking its eyes, and I knew right away that this was it—that this was the right story.

By then, though, things had changed *again*—we'd felt good about our decision at first, then had trouble getting along again and discussed the possibility of selling the car, and buying another VeggieCar, perhaps. But that changed for me the first time I held my son, looked at his shiny parts, felt him forming in my arms—making quick decisions about who he was going to be and what he would want.

"I'm going to be a social worker, a postal worker, a television cameraman," the brand new 1971 Volkswagen Beetle said to me. He read my face and listened to my chest—my heart—and said, "And I won't worry like you worry."

"Alright," I told him as I held him. "But you should know that I never planned it this way. Somehow my days turned soft. There is a limit to how many people you can hurt before it gets to you. And everything crosses over once you've been treed, and had a farm disappear on you with everything you care about inside it."

"Not for me," said the baby VW. "It is simple and beautiful."

"You could get sick and die," I said. "Cancer. Leukemia. A brain aneurysm. Sudden Volkswagen Death Syndrome."

"Not every idea is for sharing," he told me. "Just hold me and enjoy the marakesh that I am fresh and new, and I don't have a dent on me yet."

He was right. For once, I shut my mouth and my mind and focused on the new and untold story in my arms, such a gift!, and when my new baby Volkswagen shivered I held him and pulled the blanket up to his chin.

TOOLS AND SPARE PARTS

If you want to keep your Volkswagen mandarin you'll need a few tools. I'd recommend starting with the list below.

- BioLegs, one pair (for those times when the VW is being repaired, is at school or is out with friends)
- One Headless Syracuse, inner or placed
- At least two spare memory coils
- History-resistant wrenches (This is a must!)
- Spare morning cables (various lengths)
- Time (And not just any time—time you're *able to spend.* How much depends on the car and the task, but you won't get anywhere without at least a few years handy.)

Your Volkswagen will need constant repair. As confident and charged as my son was, for example, he always needed something. He was born with a cough and a limp and lesions on his skin, and he became exhausted easily, even at two or three years old. I learned early on that repairing him was not an occasion, but part of what it meant to parent this particular car. I don't even want to think about the hours this took—between the finicky cylinders, a recurring coil problem and regularly-scheduled maintenance, at least a few mornings a week. And I remember spending a *full day* reading a complicated pedal chart just to change one cranky sustain.

You'll make the coding that much more difficult for yourself, too, if you don't have a quality set of tools. My melody on tools is that it's absolutely worth going the extra hours for the good ones. You'll see cheaper coats in the stores that speak the same language, but those few extra hours will get you a better attitude or emotional state. The cheaper tools are less optimistic, they don't pray, they eat with their mouths open. Will they *believe* in the 1971 Volkswagen Beetle, the CityDogs, a story called Faces? I can't guarantee it (Though it depends, in part, on how your believer's set up.). I've had real corners with cheap tools, usually because they're so fragile. Remember, you're not just buying metal or mesh here—you're accepting a history, a group of stories that will become part of everything they touch: you, your Volkswagen, your home (via the floor of the VW's garage/room!).

I remember once, I was changing the tuning valve and harmony gauge on my Beetle—this was several months after the Lady from the Land of the Beans left, and by this point I was overwhelmed by the amount of work the VW required—with a ratchet that I'd bought at the flee bee in Hadley a few weeks earlier. As it turned out, the tool was very unstable. It had been overly chatty all afternoon—telling me about its wife, its kids, a few scrapes with the law—but late in the day it became *scared*. We were struggling with two stubborn bolts when I heard the ratchet start to weep uncontrollably—I could hear him sealing and I could feel the tears on my hand. I tried to ignore it and keep working, but when he continued to cry I pulled him out from underneath the car and asked him what was happening.

"I can't—I can't do this," he confessed.

"Course you can," I told him. "We'll get it, buddy."

"No, no," the ratchet said. "This won't work."

"What won't work?"

"This project. These bolts are thirty years old. Have you looked underneath the car? It's old and rus—"

"This car is a *newborn*," I assured him.

"What?" he said. His eyes blinked furiously. "How can that be?"

"Listen," I said. "Just calm down and focus. I'll worry about the car's well-being—you just concentrate on the job at hand."

The wrench shook his head. "Maybe I'm sick," he said, and he took off his glasses and rubbed his cast-iron eyes. "I might have a virus. Do I look sick? Do I feel cold to you?"

"You're fine," I said.

The wrench closed his eyes and shook his head.

"OK," I said. "Let's get back to work, alright?"

"I can't." He curled up in my hand. "I'm sorry," he said.

"Hey," I said. I tried to uncurl him. "Hey—hey, come on. Come on—there's work to do!" I tried to pry him open but he hugged his knees to his chest.

No way was I losing a ratchet that I'd spent good minutes on to depression, so the next day I took him in to a therapist that the Lady from the Land of the Beans had been seeing before she left Northampton. I was sitting in the waiting room and booking with the VW (who'd stayed home from school that day, claiming he was ill) while the ratchet spoke to the therapist. But then the receptionist asked me to step into the therapist's office. I left the VW in the waiting room chair. "Stay right here, alright?" I told him.

The VW, who was reading, nodded.

I scanned the room and noticed three jackals sitting across from the VW. They were whispering and laughing.

I leaned in and whispered to my son. "Hey," I said.

"What," he said, without looking up.

"What's the rule about trusting strangers?" I said.

"I won't go anywhere, OK?" the VW said at full volume. "God!"

I pinched his arm. "What did I say about that expression?"

"Alright," the VW said.

"What did I say?"

"Alright, I'm *sorry*," the VW said, and he pulled his arm away.

I went into the office and there was the therapist, wearing a therapy machine on his face. Across from him sat the ratchet, sniffling and teary-eyed in his chair.

"I'm going to need to ask you some questions if it's alright," said the therapist. The therapy machine made his voice sound like a library.

"Sure," I said. I sat down.

"Harold tells me that he's been working with you to repair your son—"

"A seventy-one Beetle," I said.

"Right," said the therapist, and I could hear his machine storing my answer. "And the Beetle is ... how old?"

"Still an infant—only a few months," I said.

"The nineteen seventy-one car is your *son*, and he's only a few months old?"

60

"Right," I said.

The therapist nodded, and then he reached up and pressed a key on the machine on his face. Then he said, "And I understand you've also lost your father recently?"

I leaned forward. "Do we have to discuss that?"

"See?" the ratchet said.

"Well wait a moment," the therapist said. "Mr. _____—I don't want to pry. I understand that you're in mourning. I'm just wondering if there's a connection between what happened—"

"I just said, I don't want to talk about my father," I said.

The therapist held up his hand and nodded slowly. "OK. Yes, I understand," he said.

Then the ratchet began to sniffle and a tear ran down his cheek. The therapist turned to him. "Harold?" he said.

"Ask him about his project—about his son," said the ratchet. "Ask him how he runs and where it goes—"

"Listen," I said. "None of this is very complicated."

"Not *complicated*!" the ratchet said.

"I'm a single parent trying to raise my son—that's all."

"A car that runs on *stories*!" shouted the ratchet.

"Harold, let's relax—take a breath. OK?" the therapist said to him. The ratchet leaned back and closed his eyes and the therapist turned to me. "Mr. _____," he said. "I'd like you to tell me, if you could, about your Memories of the One Side of Your Mother."

Soon I understood what was happening. This, *again, again,* was about me—about my favorite teams, my defensive plays. "Look," I said. I pointed to the ratchet. "His condition—"

"Interesting word," the therapist said.

"Yes, *condition*," I said. "His condition has nothing to do with me."

The therapist reached his hand out towards me. "I don't know that I'm thinking so much about Harold at the moment as I am you."

"I'm not the one in need of help."

"I don't know that I agree with that, either," the therapist said.

I stood up. "You think you can figure out how I work?"

The therapist gestured towards my chair. "Try me," he said.

I laughed. "Not a *chance*," I said. "You'd be frightened. You'd tell me I'm making it up—that it's a *fiction*. And I don't want to hear that from one more person."

"This is all beginning to make sense to me," the therapist said.

"There is nothing in the world that you can do to fix me," I told him.

LIVE ART

The Memory of My Father mourned for my father in his way, the Two Sides of My Mother in theirs. In the days after the attack, the Two Sides locked themselves inside their home in Longmeadow, holding each other and smoking their fingers as the grass grew high around them and my father's orphaned junk wrestled and moaned in the garage.

Down the street, meanwhile, the poor Storrs Library—where the Two Sides of My Mother had worked—grew faint with abandon. For as long as I could remember, the Two Sides had double-handedly run the Library, One Side working the desk and the Other Side repairing books in the basement. Now the books were starved and silent and the double doors stayed locked. Over a period of six weeks, all of the books crawled off the shelves and shuffled over to the windows and doors where they died in piles, their spines broken and their pages stiff.

I didn't know this was happening, of course; I was too busy at the time trying to deal with my own results—a newborn son, a girlfriend who couldn't bear to stay. From the very beginning I was interested in how the Volkswagen worked, which part was which, but the Lady from the Land of the Beans just wanted him healthy and running.

Even in the first few months after his birth, when she was still in Northampton and we were trying to raise him together, I could tell that she was trailing on the decisions we'd made. Without a manual to work from, she and I had to figure out the procedures ourselves. And it was difficult, because we'd open the rear lid and see something different every time—once, an old man with a hat made of newspaper pedaling his bicycle down a sidewalk that wove through the cables, past the generator and towards the clutch. Sometimes the morning cables were clear and other times they weren't.

Eventually the Lady from the Land of the Beans became overwhelmed by all this—by the mysteries of this machine, part me and part her, that she had no idea how to fix or treat. One morning, after opening the engine compartment and discovering a thick green forest—vines wrapped around the coils, birds perched on the transmission—she stood up and ran her hands through her hair. "What *is* this?" she said.

I was testing a patch of moss. "What do you mean?" I said.

"What?" the VW said. "Do you see something?"

"I don't—" She paced around the VW's bedroom. "Do you recognize anything here?" she whispered.

"This appears to be peat," I said.

She was quiet.

"But that, over there. That's 'One More Night,' I think," I said.

"_____," she said. She pulled me up and we stepped back so the VW couldn't hear us. "He's *nothing* like any car I've ever seen," she said.

"What are you guys doing?" the VW said.

"That's because he's *ours*," I said warmly, and I took her hand.

She didn't say anything, but she looked down at her hand—the one I held—as it if was something she might detach and leave if she could. I didn't know at the time what that look meant, but soon enough I came to understand it as a promise.

A few weeks later, I took the VW out for a practice drive one afternoon and when I came home the Lady from the Land of the Beans was gone. I searched the house for her, then went outside. Our half-collapsed VeggieCar was gone, too.

I came back inside and asked the VW if he knew where she was. He shook his head and looked at his wheels, but his headlights were filled with condensation. I picked him up and looked at him eye level. "VW," I said. "Where did your mother go?"

The VW's eyes held actual pity for me. "She went home," he said.

I tried to laugh. "We *are* home," I said.

He shook his head. "Not for Mom."

"What do you mean?" I said.

He looked down at the floor.

"She went back to *her* home? To the Land of the Beans?"

The VW didn't say anything.

"You let her do that?" I said. "You let her go?"

"She said she had to, Dad. She couldn't stay here anymore."

"Why not?" I asked, my voice quivering. "What did she say?"

He didn't say anything else.

"You tell me what she said," I pleaded.

I maytagged at the kitchen table and the VW sat down next to me and leaned against me. I kept saying, "She loved me. She *loved* me."

My son whispered, "No. No."

It was a few days later that I went home and found the Two Sides of My Mother sitting side by side on the love seat in the living room. They were dressed in black and the room was filled with fingersmoke so thick I couldn't see a word.

The VW, meanwhile, had gone outside to help the Memory of My Father clean up the patio. I remember watching them through the window as they loaded my father's Invisible Pickup Truck with items to take to the town dump. My father, had he been alive, would have hated it—he saw good and promise in each item that his Memory now threw away—the two-wheeled stroller (which he would have made into a wheelbarrow), the seatless bench (which he would have fixed), the neon beer signs.

I tried to make the Two Sides of My Mother feel better by commenting that it'd be nice to have more space on the patio, that we could plan a meal or a party out there now, but they weren't saying anything. They just stared past the patio and into my father's garden, where my father used to spend a lot of his day and where a pack of deer were now praying—deer prayers for the dead, I assumed.

After sitting with the Two Sides for an hour or so I remembered that it was Thursday, normally a work day for them, and it occurred to me that I hadn't heard about Storrs in weeks. "Hey Mom," I said. "What's happening with the library?"

I had to ask the question several times. They were so lost in the fog of death that I think it was hard for them to even hear my voice. But finally the Other Side of My Mother turned to me and asked, "*What* library, honey?"

It was less than a mile away, so the VW and I walked over. As we approached it, I could see that the old colonial building was now lying on its side and that the parking lot had now turned into a southwestern desert, complete with cacti and unbearable sun.

I unlocked the door but had to push hard to open it even a crack. As soon as I did I could smell the decomposing books inside.

I've always wondered: Why do so many things have to die in this book, and why is there always that *smell?*

The VW held his nose. "Why do so many things die in this book, and why is there always that same *smell?*" he said.

"Just help me push, will you?"

He did; we pressed against the door until we could open it enough to squeeze inside.

As a child, this library had been a real home for me. I remember running through the rooms as a boy with my brother and the distant Promise of the VW, getting drunk off the books as a teenager—hiding among the shelves and pressing those secret words against my eyes.

I realize now: I *couldn't* agree after that. How could I, after all the mechanical work I'd done on my own mind—the carving and slicing and reshaping? I'd liquidated tissue, pulled some wires out and used them to reconnect things in new ways. I'd told no one, either; it was secret surgery.

I remember, too, all the time I spent with the Two Sides of My Mother—sitting at the desk with One Side as she checked out the books, helping the Other Side in the basement as she operated on those volumes that were sick or dying (watching her steady hands as she made tiny incisions in the books' skin, the wordoil that sprang onto her arms).

Now this place was cold and dark, empty as a kite. The VW and I walked the halls on the first floor and then climbed up to the second, checking the pulses of the books strewn across the shelves and the hard-wood floors. All I wanted—all that I had *ever* wanted—was to find something alive, but that wasn't going to happen here. This place was a tomb.

In the midst of checking the last room for survivors, I turned around and realized that the VW was no longer behind me. I called his name, and when he didn't respond I retraced my steps. At first I was upset—he was always wandering off, getting lost!—but that feeling disappeared when I saw where he was. I found him standing at the top of the second floor balcony, his hands wrapped around the banister, his head hung and his eyes staring down at the shelves of dead magazines on the lower level. I could tell when I saw him how overwhelmed he was—his face was an underground tunnel to free the slaves.

I stood next to him without saying anything. Then I said, "I think they're all dead."

"Why," he said, without looking at me.

"I just checked all the rooms," I said softly.

"But why did it happen?" he said. "Why did they die?"

I felt almost like a real father. "I don't know," I said. "I used to ask that same—"

"*Everything* has to die, doesn't it," the VW said. "You, and me too." His eyes were dim—either on a low setting or else turned off completely.

I wasn't sure how to respond to that, but then I thought of something the Other Side of My Mother used to tell me, an old twig I'd long since stepped on and snapped. "It's only the body that dies, VW," I said. "The soul," I said, etcetera.

"I don't want to die," he whispered.

"Kiddo," I said. I picked him up and chucked him on the chin. "These books were old. They were ready to die."

The VW scanned the magazines, some of whom had leapt to the floor and died with their arms or legs outstretched. "They were?"

"Sure," I lied. "Look at their faces."

"But I'm young and new," the VW said. His eyes brightened. "Look at *my* face."

"Right—"

"And you have the *tools*, right? To repair me if anything goes wrong?"

"Most of them," I said.

The VW's face grew stern. "And you know what you're doing?"

"Absolutely I do—I'm writing a book of power on Volkswagens," I said.

"So why can't you just make sure?"

"To keep writing?"

"To keep me *going*. To make sure I don't break down or ever get old or die."

"Well—I'm—I mean, that's why I spend so much time maintaining you, buddy. To make sure you're running right."

"You promise?" the VW said. His face was now a holiday, a free give-away.

"Promise what?"

"Promise that I won't die?"

I didn't say anything. My mind stalled. I hated the idea that the VW was worrying about this *now*. He was just a child, for god's sake.

"You promise, Dad?"

The high-beams of light in those eyes—I would have said anything to keep them shining.

IV. HOW TO DRIVE A VOLKSWAGEN

TRANSMISSION

Transmission from *whom*, though?

From the Chest of Drawers, my friend and former professor, who taught Religious Studies at Northampton University. We used to go hiking up Summit Mountain in Hadley. And if we didn't, I always wished that we would have—that I'd really had a friend named the Chest of Drawers, that there really was such a thing as Summit Mountain (with a museum inside which told stories of the old cable-car hotel that used to stand in its place, and a monument to a group of soldiers who'd crashed their plane into the mountains), that there was such a thing as Hadley, or America, or me.

When the VW was old enough I took him with us, but it was always problematic when I did. When he was younger the VW couldn't keep up, and when he was older he was ill all the time, never strong enough for the hike. He would have to stop and rest, or I'd look back and find him leaning against a tree. Once, in his last year of life, I remember he stopped halfway up the trail, knelt down by a brook and vomited black, chunky oil into the running water.

But what was I supposed to do? I was a single father to a Volkswagen—I couldn't just leave him in the parking lot by himself. So the Chest and I made do; sometimes we'd slow our pace down so that he could keep up, and othertimes I'd carry him on my shoulders.

The clearest transmission that I can remember, in fact, happened late in the summer of '03, on one of our first hikes with the Volkswagen. I hiked the first half-mile with the car on my shoulders, but then he grew rambunctious and started asking to be put down. When I said no he started banging his heels against my chest.

I told him to stop it. "I'm only doing this because I don't want you falling behind," I said.

"I *won't*," he said.

"You say that now," I said, "but I know you, kiddo. You'll wander off."

"_____," said the Chest.

"He gets distracted very easily," I told the Chest. "Maybe on the way down, VW. OK?"

"We'll just keep an eye on him," the Chest said.

"Yeah! You'll keep an eye on me," the VW said.

I slowed down and leaned in close to the Chest. "But what if we lose him and the mountain changes?" I whispered to him.

"What do you mean?" the Chest of Drawers said.

What did I *mean*? This was in mid-September; the leaves had suffered and were now lying dead on the trails. Even so, you had to keep watch over this mountain, like all mountains, at all times. You didn't want to give it a chance to change its mind—to transform into a fjord or a roller rink. Such shifts made hiking (not to mention booking! How can I describe something if I don't know what it is?) almost impossible.

The key was keeping it straight in your own mind. It *was* September. The leaves had suffered and *were* lying dead on the trails.

"We just have to keep a close eye on it," I told the Chest.

"I will, I told you," the Chest said.

"The key is keeping it straight in our minds," I said.

The Chest nodded and raised his fist. "I shall pray for it, _____," he said.

By that time we were in view of the plateau at the top of the mountain and the Summit House, a museum dedicated to height and vision. With its wide decks and clean histories, the Summit House loomed over us, its cool breath on our shoulders, western Massachusetts flapping its gaze on all sides.

I set the VW down and he ran to the stairs and started hopping up them—one at a time, then two. "Dad!" he said.

"Easy, kiddo," I said.

"Two at a time!" the VW said.

"Yup, I see," I said. The Chest and I walked up the steps, around the VW and onto the deck.

"I'm doing it," he said. "Look. See?"

"I see it, buddy," I said.

Then all three of us leaned against the deck railing and peered out at western Massachusetts—which, at that moment, looked almost real. Sure, there were wires, but most of it was grass and wood, with actual pavement along the roads and literal houses and rivers. I think back on this and wonder: Was there any hint of grey smoke in the air? Was there scenery, or anything in the margins? I can't say. My memory keeps this scene clear, and gives it sunlight and honest-to-rivet clouds.

But I do remember the VW pointing out a virus of red and grey buildings in the distance and asking me what it was. "Is that a disease? Is the land sick?" he suggested.

"Sick?" the Chest of Drawers said. "No it's not sick—"

"Well, that depends—" I said.

"That's Northampton U," said the Chest.

"That's a school, buddy," I said.

"I used to teach there, VW," the Chest said. The VW nodded, then started running his hand along the bars of the railing. I could tell that the Chest of Drawers would have liked to have told the VW more about his career, but the VW turned and skipped along the veranda.

I sat down on one of the benches and stared out at the expanse. "That's about as honest a view of things as I have ever seen," I steined.

The Chest didn't say anything. He just sat very still on the bench, looking at the view, his eyes beginning to trade.

"Chest—what," I said to him.

"I'm sorry?" the Chest said, as if he hadn't heard me.

"The expression on your face is a China House," I said.

The Chest smiled. "I'm just listening," he said.

I looked out at the green fields, the tiny bioleggers on the road below. "To what?" I said.

"You don't hear that?" he said.

"Hear *what*?"

"That sound? The pasture-chord?"

I listened. "No," I said. "I don't hear anything but wind."

"It's a song—it's being sent from over there, I think," the Chest said, pointing west.

"I can't hear it."

The Chest grimaced and shook his head. "I would share it with you if I could," he said.

• • •

A few minutes later the three of us started our walk down the mountain. I didn't carry the VW this time; I just tried to keep an eye on him. When he'd stop too long to smell or touch something—funky-shaped leaves, animal poop, paths that intersected ours—I'd call his name sternly and he'd come running.

As we continued, though, the Chest and I became engrossed in a conversation—we were talking about a mutual friend, Dancing Fingers, who the Chest told me had recently died. I was stunned—this woman was my age, and she lived less than a mile away from me in Northampton. "Why didn't anyone tell me about that?" I said.

"She was sick for a while," the Chest said.

I shook my head. "I had no idea."

Fingers had been a peer of mine and the Lady from the Land of the Beans's back in college, and as far as I knew the two of them continued to speak once a month or so by phone. I wondered why the Lady from the Land of the Beans hadn't called me or told me, or told the Volkswagen to tell me.

"It was a stomach condition," the Chest said. "Her stomach wouldn't stay, wouldn't cooperate."

"Wouldn't *cooperate*?"

The Chest shook his head. "The stomach had its own ideas about what it wanted to be."

"What did it want to be?"

"A scholar."

"Of what?"

"Of *gastrointestinal studies*," the Chest flacked, as if I should have known better than to ask.

We walked on without saying anything. Then I said, "Was there a funeral?"

The Chest nodded.

"Was it a small one?"

"No, there were a lot of people there. Didn't you read the obituary in the *Wheel*?"

"I don't know how I missed it," I said.

I was lost in a regretfog for the next few minutes of the hike, and I only came out of it because I realized that I didn't know where my son was. I stopped and looked around. "Wait a minute," I said to the Chest. "Where's the VW?"

He stopped and turned around. "VW?" he called out.

There was no response.

The Chest of Drawers and I walked back up the hill, calling his name. We found him a few hundred feet up the trail; he was just standing there and staring into the woods. "Hey," I said, grabbing his shoulder. "What did I say about staying close?"

He didn't say anything.

"Hey—" I said again, but then the Chest of Drawers said my name.

I turned.

"Look," the Chest said, and he pointed off the path.

I peered into the green rage, and after a moment I saw what had stopped the VW: About a hundred feet away, a bank and a pinball machine were intertwined and faithing against a tree, their backpacks on the ground beside them.

I crouched down next to my son.

"What are they doing?" he whispered.

The pinball machine's scoreboard was full, the bank's windows fogged. They were so involved—so cofaithed—that they didn't even know we were there.

"Come on—let's go," I said to the VW.

The VW's face joined. "Are they hurting each other?"

I took a breath. "There's risk involved, because of what they can't see," I told him. "Plus the risk of trust. But no—they're not hurting each other."

The bank whispered something in the pinball machine's ear and the pinball machine giggled.

"What are they saying to each other?" the VW said.

"They're expressing their faith, VW—sharing it," the Chest of Drawers said.

I couldn't help but stare—I was mesmerized by their faith-in-progress. My stomach began hitchhiking its way through my body, looking for beans.

Then I stood up. "Let's leave them be," I said.

"Where does the faith come from?" said the VW.

Or was it a pinball machine and a French horn fearing?

I guess it doesn't really matter.

"And what's the *point* of it?" the VW said.

I didn't know what to say to that, either. I tried to form an answer.

Just then I heard a rustle, soft at first and then louder. I looked to my left and I saw a leaf floating off the ground.

I stood up.

Another leaf floated upwards, then another.

"Oh no," I said loudly.

The bank/French horn and the pinball machine heard me, stopped their faith and froze. They studied us for a moment. Then they grabbed their clothes and bags and ran deep into the trees.

But I was no longer concerned with them—I was focused on the leaves. I pointed to one. "Don't you see it?" I said to the Chest of Drawers.

He just stared at me. "What—the wind?" he said.

"Look!" I said. Leaves were floating upwards all around us now.

Distracted by other things—the VW, the faith in the trees—I had forgotten to keep the mountain straight in my mind. I had let it go, and now it was changing, reversing itself, growing young: The leaves, as they floated back up towards the branches they'd fallen from, were turning from brown back to green.

"Grab a leaf!" I said. I ran towards the closest one and tackled it.

"_____!" the Chest of Drawers yelled.

This was western Massachusetts—unpredictable; a changing, moving bitch; a switcher of faces that always seemed to press against me. How could I have made any sort of progress here when mountains were mountains one moment and something else the next; when people were here one day and then *gone*? It—Northampton, Hampshire County—wanted me to fail, to lose, to get lost in the changing no's and news and neveragains.

Not without a fight, you shiftshaping *cunt!*

The leaf grunted and wriggled in my arms. "Get the fuck off of me," she said.

I pulled down on it. "We can't let it change its mind!" I yelled back to the Chest of Drawers and the VW. It *was* September. The leaves *had* suffered and were now lying dead on the trails.

But it was already too late—the mountain had already started to change, in my mind and the minds of others. I'd thought that if I could contain at least one piece of it I might affect the whole. But it didn't work—the leaf was just too strong. I pressed all my weight on her but still she rose. Her veins pulsed and I could feel the muscles beneath her skin. "You want to tussle—is that it?" she said.

The Chest of Drawers and the VW, meanwhile, were screaming at me—the VW yelling "Dad!" and the Chest of Drawers telling me to give in, to let go. But I could hardly hear them. I held onto the leaf as she twisted and turned. Finally, she balled up her fist and springfielded me in the face.

Her punch was an ocean. I blinked and opened my eyes just in time to see another leaf-fist smash me. I let go of her and fell to the ground on my back, and the leaf fell on top of me, straddling my chest and swinging her fists and crushing my face and my stomach. I saw helping hands above me—the Chest of Drawers and the VW, trying to grab the leaf and pull her off—but she was a fury. She shook them off and bore into me with fists like aircraft carriers. She punched right through the page!

My face never did run the same after that day. That leaf broke bones that never healed correctly. To this day, I still can't properly smile—whenever I do it's a police lineup.

THE VOLKSWAGEN IS MUSIC

The Volkswagen stores its notes, phrases and all things music in something called the **Words and Pictures Coil**, which is located in an eight-inch steel cylinder right next to the memory coil. In fact, you can find the Words and Pictures Coil by tracing the morning cables from the memory coil (the two exchange information constantly). There will be several cables to choose from; the shortest will lead to the Words and Pictures Coil.

For some reason, though, Volkswagen only installs 30 centimeters (about 4.5 wraps) of coil to the Words and Pictures Coil at the factory, which isn't nearly enough for the car to retain all the language it needs to (I've written to Volkswagen repeatedly to ask them why they can't trade one or two of the eight wraps for counterverbs or more complex rhythms, but each time I do they reply with a form letter and a bunch of Volkswagen catalogues.). You may therefore find that you need to open up the coil from time to time to remove clogged or unstuck notes, or to clear out notes you aren't using so that others can be stored. Please note: Occasional clogs aren't a sign that anything is wrong—they're a fact of any Volkswagen.

To unclog a coil, first disconnect the morning cables that attach at either side. Then undo the clasps that hold the top cover down. The cover should come right off. Underneath it you should see the first layer of copper coil. You should see some notes in there, as well as memories, dreams and off-roads.

Take your missing and flush the top of the coil. Be selective—

remember that the missing is powerful, and that anything you remove from the coil is gone for good (I've known gerunds who've tried to fix their errors by opening up their missing, reassessing the memories or notes and placing them back in the coil, but that's a very messy job. And their Volkswagens were completely confused.). Hopefully, this is enough. If not, you need to detach the coil from its housing (using a triplet-wrench with an extension to get to the bolt that holds it in place) and clean the coil more thoroughly.

Again, though, you're only looking for clogged or unstuck notes—a layered melody, an obvious dischord. Everything else stays right where it is.

TUNING

Your Volkswagen should be tuned for stories at the factory, but many owners find that their cars need retuning after a few years of roadtime. I've received letters from owners whose cars are producing off-notes or -words, and I've heard from others whose cars are flat in pitch or tuned to the wrong key. This will stilt the notes' ability to project or travel, of course, and the VW will be less likely to want to play.

There are two factors at work here. First, remember that every note/word takes time, and that you or your VW are always searching for the least costly option. The sentence is a machine, and what we're essentially talking about is swapping factory parts for after-markets. If chosen right, though, the cheap words should still vibrate at a frequency that is similar enough to the original or intended word for you to hear the suffering, joy or surprise.

Choosing such words correctly, though, is almost an art in itself. It may be that your Volkswagen runs just fine, but that you or he/she are making poor word-to-time ratio decisions. Check your words—are they turning at the right speed?

If the ratio appears correct, you may have a mechanical problem. If so, the best way to find it is to run a diagnostic on the parts employed and consider which one is the culprit. Your Volkswagen can sound out of key, first, if its sensors aren't working properly, or if the morning cables that compliment them aren't clear and sunny.

If both the sensors and the cables seem sound, check the pedals. Do they push to the floor easily (but not *too* easily)? Study the top of the pedal as you push it. Is it attached correctly to the cable? If so, the cable should be taut when the pedal is pushed in.

Or it may be that the car's just fine. Are you sure that it isn't *you* who's out of tune?

NOTE CONTROL

While you can't contain the notes, you do have *some* control. The sounds your Volkswagen emits, that is, are directly connected to a) the syntactical choices you and your VW make (the letters you choose to tie to your experiences and the word choice, sentence structure and phrasing you employ), b) the positioning of those pedals in the car that are connected to the reeds. I say more about the foot pedals later on, but for now you should realize that it's your responsibility to determine which reeds each pedal turns (as each Volkswagen is different), to label them accordingly, and to begin familiarizing yourself with the ways in which pedal control can create notes, chords and "riffs."

PRACTICE

I can't emphasize this one enough. If you want your Volkswagen to make interesting, thoughtful music—music with muscle that can transport, change the weather or beat someone up—you have to make them practice. My VW used to practice a half an hour a day. We'd practice 3/4 counts, 4/4 counts, 6/8 counts, cut language timing, senteggios and so on. The VW might find these exercises tedious, but they're exactly what you need to begin creating lively, original sentences.

I'd also suggest that your VW practice scales, a new one each week. I started my VW on the *pit* scale (pit-pot-put-pat-pet), but another good one is the *calendar* scale (calendar, centerpiece, cylinder, collateral, cutthroat), or the *student* scale (student, standart, stelling, stillpaul, *stol*). Any one will work to start with, as long as it helps the VW begin to hear words as a series of sounds, helps them understand that each word has inherent musical qualities, and helps *you* get a sense for the reeds and the pedals.

With daily practice and a little maintenance, your VW will be comfortable in any musical situation that he may find himself in.

THE MASSACHUSETTS EYE AND EAR INFIRMARY

One afternoon about two months after the VW was born, he knocked on my office door while I was working on the power. When I called for him to come in he pushed open the door, leaned into the doorway and said, "Can I have this?"

"What is it?" I said. I didn't look up—I was focused on fusing a page.

"I think it's for taking notes on," he said, approaching my desk.

I finished the page I was on and then looked up. The VW was holding a clipboard.

I put down my tools. "Let me see that," I said.

He handed it to me.

"Where did you find this?" I said.

"In a drawer in the basement," the VW said. "I didn't know if it was yours or Mom's. I asked her and she told me to ask you."

My mind soft-drinked. "This was your grandfather's," I said.

The clipboard had soft corners, and my Dad had tied a stubby wooden pencil to it with a dirty white shoelace. The VW and I flipped through the scraps of paper and I read the wild script: *Call Electrician* and *Check Out 2 Fam on Masonic* and *Bry's Lasagna*.

"Is 'Bry' Uncle Bry?"

"Sure is," I said.

"He's with Colorado, right?"

"He wasn't with him at the time," I said. "He was living by himself in Suffield. My Dad would pick up a piece of lasagna for him every Sunday, after our Clipboard Meetings."

"What's a Clipboard Meeting?"

I told him how my Dad and I used to meet every Sunday at Atkin's to gripe and tell stories.

"Gripe?" said the VW.

"It's like a complaint."

"I don't know if I have any complaints," he observed.

I smiled. "You will."

"So that's it—you'd just sit and complain?"

"Not just complain—we'd chat. About school, or our real estate projects. He'd tell me about the Two Sides of Your Grandmother. I remember telling him about your Mom when I first met her.

"And we'd sit at the same seat every Sunday—in the corner, by the window," I said. "Every week I'd arrive late, and he'd already be there waiting for me."

The VW didn't say anything for a minute. Then he said, "That sounds cool."

"It was. It was really cool."

"Can *we* have one of those?"

"What?"

"A Clipboard Meeting," the VW said.

I shook my head no.

"Why not?"

A whip cracked inside my mind. "That farm isn't there anymore," I said.

"What do you mean?"

"It's just not," I said.

"Where did it go?"

"Let's save that story for when you're older," I said.

"Well, who cares if the farm isn't there? Can't we still have a Clipboard Meeting?"

"How would we do that?" I said.

"We'll have it in the car. We'll bring clipboards and cups of chai."

I shook my head again.

"Dad," the VW said, "don't you want to continue the tradition?"

• • •

That Sunday, the VW and I woke up early and stumbled down the back steps. The VW looked back towards the doorway. "Is Mom coming?" he whispered.

I shook my head. "She's sleeping in this morning," I whispered back.

"She *always* sleeps in!" the VW hissed.

It was true—in the weeks before the Lady from the Land of the Beans left us she'd stay in bed until one or two in the afternoon, completely unresponsive, the covers over her face. Even before she was gone, she was gone.

As we stepped into the parking lot the sun was brushing his teeth in the dark. The VW said he'd drive us, but I told him no—he wasn't old enough yet. "Let's take the VeggieCar,"* I said.

The VW groaned. "I *hate* the VeggieCar," he said.

"I know you do," I said. "Just a few more weeks, though."

We got in and I pulled the rootbelt over the VW's shoulder. As I did he scrunched up his face. "What?" I said.

"It stinks in here," he said. He rolled down the window-film.

"It's rotting a little," I said, strapping myself in.

"Great," the VW said.

I turned the stem once, then twice, with no luck. I released it and pumped the petals.

"I'm telling you, Dad, I can *drive*," the VW said. "I've been practicing at school."

---

* VeggieCars were vehicles made out of genetically-engineered tomatoes, peppers, cucumbers or eggplants, grown six or seven feet high, with natural engines made of seeds. They ran well and were fueled by the rain and the sun. Their only drawback was that they lasted for just six months, no matter how well-treated or preserved. Then their doors wouldn't close, and the tires started to get soft and lumpy, and the roof turned brown, and you had to say goodbye to your VeggieCar and pay a CarFarmer to go out into his or her field of cars and pick you out another one.

"I know you have—that's not the issue," I said.

"Then what's the issue?"

"We're still a few powerpages away from your learning to drive," I said.

"Why can't we skip those pages?"

I tried the stem again and this time the stalks turned. "This thing still has a little life left in it," I said.

"My seat is all lumpy," the VW said. He touched a white substance on the dashboard. "Is this *fungus*?"

We took the shortcut to Route 47—straight down the hill to King Street, fossey onto Market, over the bridge, a quick right behind the honeymoon pizza and the abandoned hotels—then a left onto Bay, over sympathetic hills, past the Museum of Sighs.

Then I saw it, approaching on our right: the former Atkin's Farm—the familiar parking lot, the tight pastures, the meditating trees.

I expected the lot to be barren, but as we approached it I saw that it was snacking with activity. The broad patch where Atkin's had knelt was now filled with ladders and drills sipping coffee out of paper cups or smoking cigarettes, the cigarettes smoking their own cigarettes or sipping coffee out of even tinier mugs. As soon as I saw the construction I remembered reading about it in the paper—they were building a new shopping face here, the widest smile this side of Hartford.

I parked the VeggieCar in a corner spot, near the lot entrance and away from the construction, and I sat for a moment with my hands on the stem. The VW poured two cups of chai and pulled out his clipboard. "So," he said. "What do we do now? Write down what sucks?"

I didn't say anything—I just stared out at the half-built face, all traces of the farmstand quickly being erased. The Memory of My Father flickered through the scenery—one moment dressed in tired winter clothes, the next leaning back in a wooden chair in the café area—but I couldn't keep him there.

"Dad?" the VW said.

I couldn't answer him—I was held in the draft of what had happened here, how much I'd lost at this place.

"Aren't you going to write down all your gripes?"

"It's all gone," I skiffed.

"What's gone?"

"Everything."

"What do you mean?"

I didn't say anything.

"Dad, what the hell?" The VW put down his clipboard. "I thought we were going to have a Clipboard Meeting."

I was silent.

"Did it die? Is that what happened?"

"Did *what* die?"

"The farm," the VW dented. "Or change its mind?"

"No."

"Then what?"

My dumb, still heart was a requiem.

"Why don't you just tell me the story?" said the VW.

I guess I'd known all along that I would tell him. How could I not? After all, this was a Clipboard Meeting, where everything was true. And why shouldn't the VW know what happened to his grandfather?

"Listen," I said. I took a breath and let it out. Then I pointed to the spot where the wide smile was smiling. "I told you that my father and I met here every Sunday?"

"Yeah. You said that already."

"Well on this particular Sunday," I said, "I was late." I started telling the VW about that day—about the table where we sat, the Tree's attack and the hijacking. I described what happened when I arrived, what I saw and what I was told by the Dogs. I told him every theory I'd heard, every note I'd sent.

What I'm saying is, I conveyed the power's first chapter as best as I could using the imperfect and dilapidated vehicle of narrative.

As soon as I'd finished, though, I realized I'd made a mistake. I read the VW's face: It was too much, too soon. He was only a few months old! His engine was racing and his eyes were flickering. When he finally spoke, he did so with a quiet intensity. "How long ago did this happen?"

I had to think about it—sometimes money slipped through my ears.

"Two months ago," I said.

"And I was born right afterwards?"

I nodded. "Just a few days."

The VW looked out the window. "You must miss him."

"I do," I said.

"Does it make you cry?"

"The missing? When I can't meet it, sure," I said.

The VW didn't say anything—neither of us did. We just sat there in the empty lot, watching the face assemble itself.

. . .

The silence was everest. Then the VW said, "Where is he right now?"

"Who?"

"Your Dad. Is he with the Tree?"

"I told you," I said, sanding down the edges of my words. "Before the Tree stole the farm he—split him in two. He's dead."

"He's dead?"

"The Tree killed him."

"Wait. That can't be right," the VW said.

"No, it is."

The VW furrowed his brow. Then he said, "But it's *your* story."

"It's not my story—it's the *only* story."

"But can't you just change it so—"

"What do you mean, change it?" I said.

"Change it."

"Look," I said. "See that face?" I pointed across the parking lot, to the expression-in-the-making.

"Yes," said the VW.

"This just *isn't* Atkin's Farm anymore," I said.

"But—"

"It's a face, whether or not I want it to be."

"But Dad, wait a second. Think about your options here. If you just try—"

86

"Try what?" I said. "Try *what?*"

"Try feeding me a different story—one that ends *well* for a change?"

I laughed.

"What's funny?"

I shook my head. "Nothing."

"No, what is it?" said the VW.

I turned to face him. "Kiddo," I said, "these are the only stories I know."

HOW TO DRIVE A VOLKSWAGEN

CONDITION

Here we go!

TOOLS AND SPARE PARTS

- At least two free Sundays
- One coil of memorywire
- A reading-speed meter
- Skip-awareness
- A peaceful set of pliers

PROCEDURE

As I've said, driving a Beetle is an act of **reading**: You are seeing a story (the road) and you are responding (**narrative pedal, scene clutch, page-wheel**). If you're doing it right, *you* are determining your speed, direction and attitude. Your job is to mind the rules of the road (the **signs**), and to stay clear as to where you are and where you hope to get to.

In some ways, driving the Volkswagen is not so different from driving a VeggieCar. As always, you're pursuing sound—only moreso in the Beetle. The controls in the VW are mostly the same, too, save for some dashboard gauges and the pedals at your feet. Most modern-day VeggieCars have eight petals, but the Volkswagen has nineteen: six for motion, two for shifting, one for chai, one for connecting, one for marginalia and mountains, two for mothersides and one for letting go. The sequence is not always the same from Volkswagen to Volkswagen, but there should be a chart underneath the dashboard that tells you which pedal is which. And if you lose it or can't see it, you can either ask your Beetle or make a chart by following each pedal-cable to its source.

The steering controls are pretty self-explanatory, as there are only a few directions to choose from: Turn the page to the right to move forward, to the left to move backwards. Notice, too, the switch for the eyelights to the left.

If you're used to driving VeggieCars, you might expect your dashboard to tell you about cropping, rot rate, nutrient levels and so forth. But the VW's dash is different. It's made from the wood of old trees, first, with needle- and text-gauges carved into the wood.

The standard Volkswagen dashboard layout starts, at the farmost left of the car, with a measurement for **Read Speed (R/S)**—how fast you're moving forward. If you go too slow you risk stopping altogether or causing an accident with another driver. Going too fast, though, you risk injury and death. Ten thousand people die each year from driving too fast. I've had several accidents, and those experiences have convinced me that we *all* drive too fast. If we all read as if we were strapped to the front cover of our book, we'd be mindful of other readers and probably save a lot of lives. So I am saying, watch that R/S Gauge carefully.

Next to the R/S Gauge is the **WMM**—the **Western Massachusetts Meter.** In essence, this gauge measures friction (right—*friction*!)—the particular friction of that moment and the half mile or so ahead. How vivid is western Massachusetts at the moment, and what side is it showing you? It could be anything: a vending machine crossing the road; a bathtub opening its mouth and showing you the virus in its throatpipes. And keep in mind that the gauge is not specific—that it will tell you how clear the image is, but not *what* it is. Nevertheless, it's very useful on the road. I can't tell you how many times I've seen the gauge hit a red four as we came around a corner, and how glad I was that I hit the breaks when I did.

Gauges Three, Seven, Eight, Thirteen, Fourteen and Nineteen, from left to right, show you the book of power *How to Keep Your Volkswagen Alive,* the stories within stories, what is dead and what is living and where we are at any given time. Note that each of these gauges lists a separate trajectory. Want to know where we are geographically? Take a look at Gauge Fourteen: It should say "Northampton." How much do we know about the VW? Check Gauge Seven!

Occasionally, these gauges need to be reset—you'll know it's time when they start telling you that you know more or less than you actually do, that you're in Athens when you're really in Northampton, that someone is ill when they're not. Hopefully, convincing the dashboard out and pressing the reset buttons—small memory-coiled flushes—will do the trick. If not, the problem is not the gauge but something else: the cable, the floater, the sensor itself.

Chai levels are reported on **Gauges Four and Six**. If you get too low, you have no choice but to turn around, wherever you are, and head back to the Haymarket.

Gauge Five measures your relationship to One Side of Your Mother, while **Gauge Seventeen** measures that to the Other Side of Your Mother.

Gauges Nine through Twelve tell you about the various fuels in the car—the stories in front of us and those we've already burned, the amount of stories filed away in the front trunk, the approximate mileage each page will get you. Note that these gauges *do not* measure the layers of skin, stress levels, or bone density of stories—they don't tell you what we're holding onto, what we've let go of, what we believe and what we can no longer accept, what our hopes are or where (in what town, with which character) our sympathies lie. For that information, refer to **Gauges Fifteen and Sixteen.**

Gauge Eighteen is the **Castaway Meter.** This tells you exactly how far in centimeters you are from the Castaway Lounge—the distance between you and those naked, dancing plots. Some models of the Volkswagen

Beetle include a compass to direct you back there, but mine does not.

Right now? Only a few miles! Nude beliefs, here we come!

Love is measured in **Gauge Twenty**—specifically, love pressure (LP) in the surrounding area. It's normal for the gauge to read anywhere from ten to twenty percent. If it drops below four percent, though, you may have trouble—the VW may get sad, slow down or even stop altogether. If this occurs, you have to immediately find/write a story that somehow convinces him that there is more love, caring or compassion in the area than he thinks there is. I can't tell you how many times this has been a problem for us—how many trips were interrupted because I had to head into the nearest populated town to see if we could find some examples of kindness. Sometimes it just wasn't there for us to find, and in those cases I'd have to sit down and try to write something—type into the book of power, print out the sheet, feed it manually. I don't think that approach ever actually yielded more LP, but I just couldn't think of anything else to do.

SIGNALS/DIRECTIONALS

Once you know the basics (how to accelerate, stop, steer) you can really go anywhere you want to: backwards, forwards, to one side or another. It's important to remember, though, that you're not the only car on the road, and that everyone around you—the other drivers, houses and businesses, streets and gutters, western Massachusetts itself!—needs to know which direction you're heading. Are you vaulting back into what was? Turning to one future or another? Taking Memorial Drive? You can avoid costly book-benders and collisions by signaling your intent.

The good news, though, is that signaling is easy: Just hold out your left arm and point it skywards if you're reading to the right, or straight out to the left if you're reading to the left.

Let's try it. First, decide which way you intend to read.

Now, signal with your left arm.

Raise your arm higher—I can barely see it.

Yes! Now I know: You're reading to the right.

Remember, too, that you're not the only one out there sending signals. Everyone and everything that you see is maintaining an image of some sort, some picture of themselves purveyed. Signaling, then, is not just choosing any old direction—it's every message you send. It's how you walk and how you look, and it's choosing a *face*—the face of a quiet reader, the face of an angry son, the face of the Longmeadow Dump. Be mindful of the signal that you're sending, and don't be afraid to let it change as you change. It is meaningful to meet a tunnel, fall in love with it, take it home and faith. But remember that the tunnel—like you, like me—is actually a signal for something else. You might go to bed entrenched and wake up to a broom or a puddle of water.

I realize this is frustrating. It's what we're trying to stop!

THE STORY

As always, there is a story—the tale, in this case, of you or me driving a Volkswagen Beetle.

I didn't *want* to use the VW as my main means of transportation, but when the Lady from the Land of the Beans left me I had no choice—she'd taken the VeggieCar and I needed a way to get to work and around town. What else could I do? I had not a minute to spare, and every job that I could think of required me to have a car.

And it's not like I had to teach him; the VW knew everything he needed to already. He'd already practiced turns and maneuvers in the big driveway behind our house, and his teachers at school used to tell me that he'd spend his time during recess showing off his three-point turns on the playground. *I* was the one who needed the practice, and so every day for two weeks the VW and I went out for drives. I'd practice stops and starts on Crescent Street, then lag onto Routes 9 or 5 and rehearse accelerations, shifts and page-turns until I finally felt I could control the car.

But learning to drive the VW wasn't a smooth process; in fact, we fought almost every time we practiced. I'd get angry at the VW for speeding or traveling too many lines at one time, or he'd groan about how slow I was going or the fact that we traveled the same roads over and over.

And while the VW knew how to maneuver himself on the road, he didn't understand the first thing about western Massachusetts—its stops of story and memory and fear. I scolded him repeatedly for driving too casually, for not staying aware. One fall afternoon, while driving through Florence, I tried to elaborate. "There are roads that we can take and roads we can't," I explained.

"Why not?"

"Because people go down those roads and they don't come back," I said.

"Ever?"

"Right," I said.

The VW was quiet for a moment. "Well, how do we know which roads are OK?"

"I'm writing about that in the power," I told him. "The first rule, though, is to follow your ears, your heart."

The Volkswagen spoke slowly. "Follow my ears—"

"Well, your sensors."

"—and my heart."

"Your engineheart," I said.

"What am I listening *for*?"

"For change—the sound or sign of change. That's why you need to avoid the main routes. Forty-seven is OK, and five, but *never* ninety-one or ninety."

"Why not?"

"Because you can get lost; they might take you so far away from here that you'll—*we'll*—forget which roads you took," I said. "Or, Northampton could change its tune while you're driving, seal off its exit, and then you're screwed."

The VW seemed to be digesting this. "Why can other cars—"

"You're not like other cars," I told him. "They're searching for something. You already have everything you need."

How could I know at the time how true those words were?

Even so, though, the VW heard but didn't *listen*. He was always getting lost or distracted by something on the side of the road, and the older he got the more curious he became and the harder it became for me to drive him. He'd make decisions without asking me, take turns without even signaling. Once, driving towards Hadley, he saw an entrance to Route 91 and he leaned towards it as if I wouldn't notice.

"Hey," I said, grabbing the wheel.

He didn't say anything. He just kept leaning.

"VW," I said again. I yanked the steering wheel over. "What are you doing?"

The VW spat oil.

"What's the rule about ninety-one?" I said.

"Even though there are a million freaking cars on it."

"*They* aren't *you*," I said.

"You mean they aren't *sick*?"

"You aren't sick," I said. "You just don't understand—"

"—understand the area. I know."

"You don't," I said. "These towns can be loud and harsh."

"Sure they can," the VW curred.

"Alright big shot—what do you do when you meet a city made of parchment?"

The VW's eyes went off. "There are cities made of parchment?"

"Off ninety-one? Absolutely. Parts of *Amherst* are paper-thin. Not only that, I've seen towns made of prayer—heard of others made of fabric and film."

I could hear the VW processing this. "But how do I navigate—"

"You don't. You stay off ninety-one, away from the changes."

The VW made a gutterface. "Away from the changes," he sang, impersonating me.

"Hey—stop that."

"Stop that," the VW said, his voice high and thin.

"I wonder what a good memory coil would go for at the flee bee," I said.

The VW smiled and slowed down. "You wouldn't do that," he said.

"You never know," I said.

FREQUENTLY CRASHING QUESTIONS

I have trouble shifting my VW. Am I doing something wrong?

Probably not. Shifting a VW is more difficult than shifting other cars; VeggieCars allow you to shift a stalk from one seed-cluster to another, but to shift a Volkswagen you must select from twenty-five different gears spread out over five different transmissions. It simply takes money to get used to that system, and to immediately know when to use which speed.

Often, though, it's an issue of common sense. Clearly I used a faster speed—gear 4/3 (transmission four, gear three), say—for an excerpt from the manual, a lower gear for "One More Night," a higher gear for "A Scanner Darkly." I'd use a 3/1 on Route 9, a 3/5 on Route 47, a 1/4 downtown. If I switched to too low a gear—a 1/5 on 47, say—the Volkswagen would stall.

This all might be fiction, though, because usually the VW shifts for you. It's only if he fails to do so that you have to grab the page and shift it into gear.

It's a good question nevertheless, because effective shifting can increase the life of your Volkswagen Beetle. Poor shifting, meanwhile, can cut his or her life in half.

What if the Volkswagen stalls?

Don't give up! Mine used to stall all the time. If that happens with yours, close it and let it cool down. Then stand behind it and give it a push. Sometimes it's just parked on a bad phrase, and if you push it you'll ease it onto the next one and it'll start right up. Then start the car and rev it. Hopefully, forward motion will be restored.

If that doesn't work, though, there may be a more serious problem—the first phrase may be completely dead, for example, or one of the morning cables attached to the scene clutch may be clogged or stuck. For more information about this, check "Engine Stops or Won't Start" (Chapter Seven).

How can I tell if my book is still alive?

That's an easy one: Check its pulse! There is a beat on every page, so you must look through the sentences until you see it. Then put your finger on it and make sure that it's regular. You might also check under the VW's voice box, on the inside of his right front wheel, on the underside of his front storage compartment or under the driver's seat. Press your finger against the sentence. You should feel an unmistakable rhythm, a contagious waltz.

My Volkswagen is asking to go to driving school. Should I let her?
No—not to driving school or *any* school, in my opinion. It's just not necessary. My son attended the Jackson Street School in Northampton for a few months when he was a child, but he'd come home each day talking about unfamiliar eeps—mass no's and time-as-turning. When he told me about them I'd say, "Didn't they teach you anything about traffic? The rules of the road?"

The VW would shake his head and say something like, "Today we learned about the Holocaust."

I say, your VW already has everything he needs. All he has to do is go from *here* to *there*, and that's something you can teach him.

What if the story gets dark?
This does happen from time to time—light leaves the car, the book, and the roads of western Massachusetts—and no one is exactly sure why. Luckily, the Volkswagen is born with luminescent eyes that light up in accord with a) his spiritual mode, b) the position of the switch to the left of the page.

One theory on this is that Volkswagens not only emit light from their eyes, but actually *broadcast* everything in front of them—the entire page/scene. This sounds treble, I know, but I've received letters from several severances who believe that the act of reading is actually a trip through the Volkswagen's mind as sent out through his eyes.

Whose story do you think this is?
A fair question. At the center of this all, we will discover, is the question of control. Hampshire and Franklin County will present themselves, will

ask us—you, me—to change. We will have to make decisions. It will be important to know who is steering the car—you, or the VW?

The answer to that question depends very much on the situation, on where we are in the story. There are moments here where the VW is just a margin, hardly tested. Sometimes he will turn his own pages, other times he can't. In these cases, it's *your* job to take the wheel in your hands and steer the car yourself.

In many cases, you and the Volkswagen will share the job. And that's the way it should be, it seems to me. I like the idea that driving the Volkswagen is an act of cooperation—you and I working together, each of us befriending our Volkswagen and learning how to help him or her. Because in many ways, we're all the same—the Volkswagen is a machine that digests information and responds to it, and so are you. Plus we're all trying to reach the same thing (the end/home)!

It would be easy and foolish, though, to forget to make room for others' needs as well. Remember that we'll be sharing the road with pedestrians, opinionated signs and other drivers. There may very well be moments in these stories, then, when the VW wants to go one way and you want to go another, or when you've simply had enough and you want to *go*—to speed, to flee—but must stop in the name of safety and community.

For me, that's what made parenting the Volkswagen interesting and fun. I was never alone when he was alive. I was sharing in something that was larger than myself, and so are you: By stepping into the VW, turning the key and moving into traffic, you are part of a tradition, a family that spans across place and name, deep into the past and fast forward into tomorrow.

V. FLAT TIRE!

SHIMMIES AND SHAKES

That was back in the fall when everything fell—when the VW's mother, the Lady from the Land of the Beans, left us for the homefarm; when my son began to ask questions I didn't know the answers to; when the loss of my father began to burn my sidestreets. I fumbled, lost hold: The Volkswagen was no longer a newborn, and he was beginning to have health problems. And the apartments at Crescent Street—the five-unit Victorian that my father had raised and loved and run like a quite? They howled for help—help I tried, and failed, to give.

My father had bought the building, a British-speaking outburn, when I was a student of distance in the late 1990s. The house had been raped and beaten and a group of nomadic ovens had discovered it empty and moved right in. My father went in there with love and kindness and tried to heal the house, but the ovens wouldn't leave. My Dad had to appeal to the city to resolve it. I was there at those meetings, with the ovens in their headbands and dirty dresses—I remember them weeping, my father promising, Northampton extending her hand. My Dad was awarded the right to parent the house, and he did exactly what he promised the City he would; he gave all his time, every minute he could pledge or owe, to convincing the dizzy home back to grace, and went so far as to move the ovens into a small house at the edge of the property.

The project took two years of flexing to complete. I was a flipper at the time, young and two-minded, and I didn't help out as much as I should have. As I grew older, though, I became more involved in running the place.

When my father was attacked by a Heart Attack Tree in 2003, I moved into one of the apartments and vowed to do the Memory of My Father proud, to hold that house in my arms and nurse it the way my

Dad would have wanted me to. But then my son was born, and there just wasn't enough time to go around. Every week I was spending four or five hours at least on parts for the car. That might not sound like a lot, but it adds up! New front sensors run anywhere from fifteen to twenty hours a pop, and the custom break system cost me sixty-five hours alone! I probably visited one store or another—ParentParts, Faces, Northampton Custom Auto—at least every other day for something for my son.

At the same time, the house was o'reillying—the sinks moaning, the heaters rumpering, the wires in the walls gnashing their teeth. Winter was coming and I didn't have a single moment in my pocket. Plus, my Volkswagen was getting older—old enough, now, to drive—and that required time as well; time for tires, time for bulbs, two hours a morning for booking for fuel (maintenance, documentation, narrative, you name it!).

One day, desperate for time, I went down to Faces and sold my name. But the time they gave me for it lasted us a little less than a week.

Then I heard that the *Daily Wheel* was looking for a reporter, which is another word for a fontana, a person who works with words. So I went to their offices on Conz Street and I sat down with an editor, a small block of cheese named Louise. I showed her my schoolscars and my writing-torn wrists and she read some of my buildings.

After a few minutes of reading she looked up from the page. "And you have a car?"

"A son? Yes," I said.

"And it's dependable?" she said.

"When he's in the mood to be, yes," I said. I laughed, but Louise stared at me like a wood-burning stove. "Yes," I said.

The next morning I woke the VW up early and told him that he wouldn't be going to school that day. Instead we drove down Route 9, onto Conz Street and into the *Wheel* parking lot. The VW pulled into a space next to a line of cars that were for some reason (they were either sleeping, shy or dead) completely silent.

"What now?" the VW said as he slowed to a stop.

"What?" I said. "I've got to go inside."

"And what am I supposed to do?"

"You stay here," I said.

"For how long?"

"I don't know," I said. "I'll probably be out in a couple of hours."

"Oh, come *on*," the VW said. "You want me to just sit here? Why can't I go back to school?"

"Because I need you for transportation," I told him, closing the driver's side door and walking towards the office entrance.

"When do I go back?"

I turned around. "If this job works out, I don't know that you *will* go back to school," I said. Then I pointed at him. "Take notes on everything you see."

"This *sucks*," the VW said.

I can still remember the offices of the *Wheel,* the way the place reverberated and turned, the feeling of those words against my lips, still warm from the pressing. I remember, too, how good it felt to be there, out of that howling house and *doing* something. It was only when I got away from the apartments that I realized how much of a toll it took on me to keep them going. I was living in a structure of loss, and as I breathed in that loss it was changing me. I rarely tasted my food. Sometimes I'd open up a book and all the words would be the same.

But writing for the newspaper turned out to be much harder than I thought, and Louise had her hands full trying to teach me the basics. We spent hours at her desk reviewing articles together, talking about how they were built—where to put the front door and the porch lights and the plumbing.

"See, these things don't really work like fiction does," she explained, pointing at the printout with her cheese-arm.

"You mean, like fuel?"

She blinked my question away. "What I'm saying is, everything in here is true."

"The engine is true, too," I said, snapping my suspenders. "True as in, *literal.*"

"Look," she said. "See how this story cascades from the top down, with the most important information first?"

"I love that idea, of words

cascading," I said.

"And check out the lead," she said, pointing to the first line. "See its teeth?" She read my face, the power that had appeared. "No—lede," she said. "L-e-*d*-e."

My face changed.

"Are you with me?" she asked.

"Absolutely," I told her.

I learned from Louise that a story is nothing more than a series of events, and also that a reader cares more about a story when they see themselves in it. This was totally new information for me. Was this why the VW was ill all the time—because people couldn't see themselves in the fuel? Or because more needed to happen?

A few days later I was sent out on my first official story: Somehow Main Street in Northampton had transformed from a street to a canal. Louise called me in the middle of the night and told me to get down there and find out what had happened—how the streets had filled, who was hurt, if anyone had been killed and what would happen now.

I said I'd be right there.

"Sorry if I woke up your wife, by the way," she said.

The closest thing I had to a partner in those days was a future pile of shattered glass. "No no," I told her, "I am completely alone."

She said she'd see me in the morning and we hung up. I thought fast: Canal. Volkswagen.

I picked up the cordless phone, busked down to the basement and called the Memory of My Father. It was four in the morning. I didn't have a ready memory of talking to my father that late, though, so the voice that answered the phone was the one I heard whenever I called around 11:30, just after my Dad went to bed. If I called that late my Dad would know it was me, and he'd answer the phone without asking who it was. "What's up," the Memory of My Father said when he picked up.

"Dad," I said. "Didn't we used to have an outboard motor somewhere down here?"

He thought about it for a minute. "Jesus, _____—I don't have a clue," he said. "I can look next time I'm up there."

"I need it now," I said.

"You need it right this minute," he crullered.

"I do—for a story," I said.

"*Cris*," he swore.

"Wasn't it in the room with the furniture?"

"I moved it," the Memory of My Father said. "How about under the worktable?"

I took the phone into the dusty, junk-filled workshop and turned on the lights. Bugs scurried in every direction, swearing and muttering insults.

I looked under the table. "I don't see it," I said.

"How about the boiler room?"

I went into the boiler room—all five burners were humming in the modal key of heat. I stepped between them. "Where?" I said.

"The only place it could be in there is behind those drop tiles," the Memory of My Father said.

I pushed a pile of drop ceiling tiles over and saw the motor in the corner, leaning against the brick and covered with a thick layer of pink dust. "Found it," I said.

"It's there?"

"I have it right here," I said.

"Son of a bitch," the Memory of My Father said. "Talk about a lucky guess."

"Sorry to wake you," I said.

"Not a problem," the Memory of My Father said, just like my father would, and he hung up the phone.

I dusted the motor off, carried it upstairs and leaned it against the wall outside the VW's bedroom door. Then I knocked. "VW," I whispered.

He was snoring, loudly.

"VW," I said in a normal voice.

I heard him stop snoring. He murmured something unintelligible.

"Gotta wake up, buddy."

"Dad! What time is it?"

"There's a story downtown," I said. "We need to go."

I heard shuffling across the floor, and then the VW opened the door. "I'm sleeping!" He was dressed in pajamas and his eyes were almost completely dark.

"I know, kiddo," I said. "But there's a story—"

"Can't you just walk?" he said.

"With the power?"

He threw his arms in disgust. "I can't believe this," he said, rubbing his eyes. "It's totally—" Then he saw the motor leaning against the wall. "What is *that*?" he said.

. . .

The night was amazingly, astoundingly *dark*. I carried a jigsaw, a screwgun, some tools and the motor. The VW trailed behind me.

"This is crap," he said. "It's the middle of the night!"

"I can't control when things *happen*," I told him. "All I can do is respond to them, alright?" I stopped and told the VW to stand still and I placed the jigsaw against the metal.

"Well it's lame, Dad," he said. "I finally get to drive and all I do is taxi you all over town."

"I'm trying to concentrate, alright?" I barked, and I pulled the trigger on the jigsaw and began cutting a small hole in the VW's engine panel.

"Ouch!" the VW said. "That freakin' hurts."

"That's why they call it a *job*," I said between my teeth. "No one said it would be fun."

"If it's your job, why am I the one getting cut?"

When I finished cutting out the square, I drilled pilot holes at the corners. Then I fastened the motor to the sheet metal. It fit almost perfectly, but the VW complained that it was too heavy. "How am I supposed to drive with this thing?" he brumbled.

"I don't have time to go through every detail with you right now—it's my first assignment and the story's getting cold," I told him. "You're just going to have to figure some things out on your own, alright?"

I took a spare morning cable from the VW's storage compartment and ran it from the distributor to the second transmission. Then I started up the car, told the VW to stay still, and got out to check the outboard motor. Pure as pork, its blades were spinning.

I stood back. "Hey. Not bad, huh?"

The VW shook his head.

I got in and we pulled out of the driveway and down Crescent, the outboard motor bouncing and finning as we tore through the pre-dawn. We drove out to 9, took a left and approached the city center. As we came down the hill towards Main Street I could see the water line; it crept right up to the steps of the Academy of Music. Main Street, I saw, was completely submerged.

"Are you serious?" the VW said, staring at the water.

"Didn't I tell you?" I said. "It's like I'm always saying, you've got to be ready for anything. You can't just assume things will stay the way you remembered them."

"No shit," the VW said.

"OK—you ready?" I said. I pressed the narrapedal to move us forward.

"No—wait a second, wait a second!" the VW said. We stopped abruptly. "I can't do this, Dad—I'm not a *boat!*"

"Just read the water and stay open to it," I said. "Think very buoyant thoughts. And stay close to the curb, alright?"

The VW didn't say anything.

I checked his fuel gauges. "You have enough fuel?"

"Right this minute? Plenty," he said sarcastically.

"OK," I said. "Release the break, will you?"

"*You're* on the pedals," he said.

I shook my head. "They're all the way out—it's your fear, not mine," I said.

Slowly, the VW let go of his fear and we eased towards the water. As he inched forward it covered his wheels and headlights, then rose to his fenders and almost to the windows. I felt the wheels leave the ground and the motor kick in—it kept us afloat and pushed us forward through the darkness.

I was immediately proud of myself. "You see?" I said to the VW. "Your Dad knows what he's doing, doesn't he?"

"Isn't this really bad for my skin?" the VW said.

"Why do you always have to focus on the negatives?" I said. "Anyway, I don't see why it would be—it's no different than swimming in a pool or going through a carwash. Is it?"

"Those things aren't good for my skin, either," the VW said.

"Bah—you're fine," I said.

It was clear as we moved down Main Street that there wasn't much happening yet; some CityDogs were standing on the sidewalk, staring at the water that ran from curb to curb, and a crane was shining its lights down into the black water and lifting cars out onto the sidewalk. But that was it—the stores were closed and the sidewalks were still sleeping.

I steered us past Cha Cha Cha and the Mercantile and towards one of the CityDogs on the curb. When we coasted up next to him I grabbed my book of power, *How to Keep Your Volkswagen Alive*, pulled myself through the driver's side window and up onto the sidewalk and asked the City-Dog if I could speak with him. I told him I was _____, that I was reporting for the *Wheel*. I held the book up to his face. "Can you tell me what happened here?" I said.

"Street filled with water," he said. His eyes were glazed and he was eating a piece of fruit.

"Does anyone know how it happened?"

"Nope," he said.

I could hear the engine of my book turning as it recorded his testimony.

"And what's being done about it?"

He took another bite of his fruit, and when he did I saw what it was. This Dog was eating a *Kaddish Fruit*—a grown prayer, a religious high. "Right now we're just trying to clear out the street," he said. "Mayor Statue-of-Coolidge is supposed to address the town later today."

"Do you know what time?"

"Don't think they've announced it," the CityDog said.

I tried to think of more questions to ask, anything to get at the story, but I was distracted by the fruit in his hand—the color of it, a violent blue. I lowered my power book and looked into the Dog's eyes. His corneas were soft as pillows.

He stared back at me. "What?" he said.

I pointed to his paw, the Kaddish. "Mind if I ask where you got that?"

He smiled. "You can ask," he said.

"There used to be a field of those near the house where I grew up," I told him. "I didn't think they grew around here anymore."

"Well," he grinned, "they do."

"I could use one or two, you know?" I whispered.

"Who couldn't?" the CityDog said.

"No, I mean I'm in a particularly bad lane right now. My father was killed by a tree not so long ago, his body driven off."

The Dog pointed at me with his paw. "Those orchards out near Hampshire?"

"Yeah—Atkin's," I said.

"Sure, I worked that case," the Dog said. "That was your Dad?"

I nodded.

"Man—I remember how *bare* that place was when we got there." He shook his head. "Those trees strike and fucking *vanish*. Seen it happen a bunch of times. Anyway," he said, looking down at his boots. "I'm sorry about it."

I looked down at the VW. He was treading water and pleading with his eyes for us to go.

"Hey," the Dog said. "Can you keep a secret?"

I turned the book of power off. "Of course I can," I said.

The Dog leaned over and whispered in my ear. I could smell the prayer on his breath.

• • •

I handed in the story that afternoon, and I stood by Louise's desk as she read it over. But she didn't even get past the first line—the *lede*. She slapped the page with her cheese-wrist and looked up at me. "What is this supposed to be?" she said.

".What do you mean?" I said.

"Why am I reading about a grove of Kaddish Fruit trees here?"

I happened to have a fruit with me at the time, and I took a bite from it. "The CityDog gave me *directions*—it's out behind the high school. I went and saw it myself—rows of them, perfectly ripe, all shining and commanding. I saw it and thought, 'Now *there's* a story!' You know, we used to have a grove of these in the town where—"

"_____. Where's the story about the canal?"

"There wasn't much *to* that story. No one knew why the streets had filled. And they're not doing anything to fix it."

"The fact that the streets filled with water *is* the story," she told me.

"How is that a story?" I said.

Louise held out her hands. "Something strange and unexpected happened—that's newsworthy," she said, her voice curbing and turning.

"But it's just a change-and-changeback. The Kaddish one had long-lost religion. Discovery. Nature!"

Louise ran her cheese hands through her cheese hair and looked down at her notepad. "The Statue of Coolidge is holding a press conference at four—I want you there," she said.

I nodded reluctantly and took another bite of my fruit.

Louise looked up at me. She pointed to my hand, the fruit-bodied prayer. "What is that?" she said.

"This?" I said. Everything felt free.

"Is that what I think it is?"

I smiled. "What do you think it is?"

"Don't even tell me," she said.

. . .

Needless to say, I had a lot to learn about journalism. After a little more than nine months, several failed assignments, and a number of disagreements over what was or was not a story, I left the *Wheel* and decided to dedicate myself to the Crescent Street apartments—to revive them, rent them, do my father proud.

But that didn't work either. I just didn't know enough. I could tell you a lot about Volkswagens, but home repair was a different screen altogether. I didn't understand plumbing, couldn't wrap my mind around the fundamentals of electricity. A pipe on the first floor burst, and then the burners downstairs broke and I couldn't fix them. In the years that followed, I sold off every attribute inside them piece-by-piece in order to raise the time to take care of my son.

The story of the 57 Crescent Street house doesn't crescendo, but fades out instead: Later, a few months after the death of my father, I finally ran out of options and time. I had to sell the place to my brother, the schoolteacher.

By that point the house was empty, and I was living in Deerfield with the Museum. One winter morning, my brother and I met at the house to finalize the deal. Neither I nor the Museum had been able to afford to keep a car or a bio, so I rode her bike all the way from Deerfield to Northampton for the meeting. By the time I got there my nose was a single vowel, nothing more.

Bry and I hadn't spoken face-to-face in, I don't know, years. As I stood there waiting for him I lit the fingers on my left hand and smoked them. The keys to the house wept into the pocket of my coat. "*Please*," one of them said.

"Shut up," I whispered, breathing fingersmoke into the amazing air. "There's nothing I can do."

Then my brother showed up in his Honda. He was older now; his eyes were closets and he was starting to lose his hair, like I had long ago. He met me on the steps and put his hand out. I handed over the keys without saying a word, stepped off the porch, got on my girlfriend's bicycle and pedaled down the sidewalk and through the snow.

HOW WORKS A HEART ATTACK TREE

CONDITION

There's no need to pocket because I know why you're here: You want to know why and how a Heart Attack Tree works, why it would kill your mother—your father, your children—when it will strike again, where it lives and what we can do to stop it. You're sick of the fucking *changes*. And so am I.

THE STORY

I may not have given in to the VW's pleas to tell stories of traversing across western Massachusetts to look for the Heart Attack Tree, but I didn't just accept the Tree's crime either. I did what I could, first, to learn about Heart Attack Trees. Just a few days after I told the VW the Katydids, I took him over to the Smith College Library so we could do some research.

But our findings only echoed the Dogs' claims: These trees were born with a powerful craving for story and heart, which they can smell in a human being's chest. They eat the heart to get to the muscle, the story. Without concord nourishment, though, the tree grows foggy and "wanders around in a drug-like state, exhausted and confused."* I learned that there are seventy-four breeds of Heart Attack Tree in America, and over fifty additional breeds in Europe. In the U.S., apparently, the Heart Attack Tree's best weapon is anonymity; either they stay hidden in the woods, trying not to be noticed, or they enroll in the Federal Heart Program (FHP), which entitles them to three artificial hearts per day. (In Europe, incidentally, *all* Heart Attack Trees must register, and are branded with a ring around their trunk. Subsequently, many British Heart Attack Trees live in exclusive communities—pulmonary forests—in order to avoid public scorn.)

---

* Cimarron Ash, "Nutrition and the Heart Attack Tree," *The Journal of Arboreta Craveotus* 6, no. 1 (1980): 65.

One power, though, elaborated further on the makeup of these "Heart Attack
Hearts"; apparently they're made from paper, and bound with glue, an
while most Heart Attack Trees attest that they taste sort of heart-like,
they're not nearly as savory or nourishing as the real thing.* They do
help reduce attacks, though, and the FHP has a system in place for rep-
rimanding those trees that do attack: They either lobotomize them, re-
locate them, or both. But they're extremely hard to track. Many Heart
Attack Trees remain fugitives because they never bothered to register with
the FHP to begin with; this makes them almost impossible to identify or
pick out of a lineup.

Plus, you never know whether you have the tree or its Memory!

The VW and I also started surveying the area. For a while there when
I was working at the *Wheel* we stole away almost every afternoon, drove
my VW into Amherst and spoke to anyone who might have seen a tree
driving a farm. I interviewed houses, trees, 116 itself. ("I've seen farms
driving along here from time to time," the road told me, "but I never
thought to look inside them and see who was at the wheel.")

Then, one day in the spring of '05, I tracked down a tree who matched
the general description, and who'd reportedly gone missing just around
the time that my father had.

That afternoon, the VW and I were driving through South Hadley
when the VW had a hankering for chai. He began begging for it. I was
on my way out to Mount Holyoke to interview an amphitheatre about
a lawsuit, but the VW was beligerating—slowing down, whining, stopping abruptly. "So thirsty," he gasped. "Need chai."

"Stop it," I told him.

"Can't—parched. Need ... milk and ginger," he said.

I custom-swore at him and told him no, but finally I had no choice—
he wasn't going to keep going if I didn't find him some chai soon. Luckily, the Thirsty Mind Café was right off 47 in the Village Commons, so
I pulled over, grabbed my bag with my wallet inside and ran upstairs to
the café.

As I was waiting at the café counter, though, I noticed a glass case in

---

* Red D. Cedar, *Paper for Breakfast: A Survivor's Story* (New York: Daisy Press, 1994), 23.

front of me with some bulges of plastic beneath it. When I looked closer I saw a purple organ with blue arteries beneath the plastic. These were actual fake hearts, I realized, and expensive ones, too—two hours a pop, according to the piece of paper next to them.

When I think now about what my *father's* heart was worth—how many hours!

"Those hearts?" I asked the typewriter behind the counter.

He nodded. "Made by Pothole Pastries. They're good."

"They for trees?"

He nodded.

"Sell a lot of them?"

The typewriter shook his head. "Barely any. They're big with some breeds, but we don't get so many trees in here anymore. There used to be one, he'd come in almost every day on break."

"He doesn't buy them any more?"

"He doesn't come by—he hasn't been here in months," the typewriter said.

As subtly as I could I reached into my bag, turned on my book of power and pushed the button for it to record. "How come?" I said.

The typewriter looked at me skeptically. "Can I get you a coffee or something?"

I reached into my wallet and slipped an hournote across the counter.

"What's that?" the typewriter said.

"That's time. For information about that tree."

"What for?" the typewriter said.

I slipped another note to him. "Because I like trees."

"There are plenty of—"

"I'm interested in *this particular* tree," I said.

"Like I said, he doesn't come in anymore. But he had lambchop sideburns. These heavy, drooping eyelids."

"Did you ever see him driving a farm?"

The typewriter stared at me. "What?"

"A farm," I said.

"I only ever saw him when he came in for coffee. I think he works at

Fedora's—sometimes he came in wearing an apron."

I shook my head—I didn't know the place.

"It's a restaurant and bar. Right around the corner."

"And he stopped coming by?"

The typewriter nodded. "A month or two ago, maybe."

I made a note in my power: *Fedora's*. "Anything else I should know about this sideburned tree?" I said.

The typewriter crossed his arms. "You aren't going to hurt him, are you?"

I leaned against the glass case and studied the wrapped hearts. "Ever try one of those?" I asked.

"Me? No."

I tapped my fingers on the glass. "Let me get one to go. And a medium chai."

The typewriter took out a pair of tongs and pulled one heart out of the case. "That'll be three hours."

I looked deep into my wallet. I heard screams. I saw a tongue wagging. Finally, I saw four hours balled up in the corner. I handed them over and the typewriter put a paper cup on the counter and placed a heart in my hands.

Outside I met the VW and we sat down on an iron-wrought bench. "What took you so long?" the VW said.

I handed him his chai. "That café sells hearts," I said.

The VW wrapped his hands around the cup and took a slow sip. "Yes," he said. "Yeah, mama. Good old American *chai*," he smoothed.

I set the heart down on my lap and opened up the wrapping. Inside was a stack of paper, bloody and bound.

"What are you doing?" the VW said.

I sniffed the heart—it smelled sour, like blood.

"Dad—what are you doing?"

I shrugged. "I'm curious—aren't you?"

"About what?" Then the VW's face changed, and I could tell he realized what I meant. "Oh, Dad. Please. Don't tell me."

"Just a bite," I said.

"Ugh," the VW said, resting his cup of chai on the arm of the bench. "Why not?" I said. "It's not like it's real—it's manufactured."

The heart was cold to my lips and it tasted like paper. I took a bite of it, swished it around in my mouth. It was freezing cold, and slippery. It had the texture of the sole of a shoe. It was very tough to chew and swallow, but I did my best.

The VW was obviously put off. He leaned back and his face lost its blue color. "Why in the world would you *do* that?" he said.

• • •

That whole experience turned out to be a wild tree chase, though. I spoke to Fedora's and they told me that the tree was on leave, but after some additional elsing at the *Wheel* I found out why: He'd been admitted to Holyoke Hospital a month earlier. He had testicular cancer—a cyst in his right testicle, which he'd thought was benign, turned out to be a tumor. He went in to get it looked at, but by then it was too late.

FLAT TIRE!

PROCEDURE

Flat tires are perhaps one of the more serious emergencies that you'll encounter with your VW. If your son or daughter gets one, the best thing to do is to pull them off of the road, sit cross-legged on the car and wait for help.

I have received countless letters asking whether fixing tires is something that one can do oneself, and the answer is *NO!* I have known vulcanizers to do it, but some of those *same* vulcanizers have crashed their children because their tires were running on voided, cancelled messages.

Tires are simple devices made out of rubber, with tubes inside filled with breath. But not just *any* breath. Volkswagen sends out nomads whose sole job is to find drivers/parents with flat tires, heal those tires and breathe them full. These are the people that you're waiting for. You might sometimes see them walking alongside the road, their hands dirty and their feet rolled. I have known people who waited two *days* for one to arrive, but once they're there they can fix the tire within three or four hours tops.

THE STORY

I have only had this happen to me once (thank god!), when I was lost with the VW in Wilbraham. The road happened to be taking a nap at the time. It turned over in its sleep and its fingernail punctured the right rear tire.

I heard the tire go and the VW said a custom-made swear. I pulled over to the side of the road, got out of the car and debated whether to try and change the tire myself. But I didn't know where to start—how to get the tire off the car, even.

So I did the only other thing I could: I climbed on the back of the VW and I sat there with my legs in an X. The sun beat down on me. I heard frequencies in the air—person-to-persons, distance jams, other books of power. I tried to be still.

Later that evening the Volkswagen nomad arrived. I saw her condensing down the road, her body like a game. Even from afar I could see her VW action suit, the insignia emblazoned on her chest. As she approached I saw that her hair extended to her ankles, and that half of it was natural and the other half mechanical. The mechanical strands moved on their own.

I hopped off the car and the nomad took the VW in her arms as if she were his mother. She held him and breathed into the flat tire. It only took a few minutes—only one or two continuous breaths, actually—to inflate the tire completely. I watched everything she did and I still have no idea how she did it. Before I knew it she was finished, and the VW was standing there ready to be driven.

This nomad's face was beautiful, and my thoughts were grazing. I offered her time of money, but she must have seen a pause in my eyes because she held her hands up and refused. I tried to talk to her, to start a conversation, but I'm not sure that she'd been given a voice to respond with. If she did, she didn't use it with me. I managed to thank her and that was it; as quickly as she arrived she was gone, walking down the side of the road as the hot sun ridiculed above, her long hair crinkling and chirping as she went.

LOOK BACK IN ANGER

The Memory of My Father was born at Atkin's in the clutch of the Tree's escape. Or, he was born in the days afterwards, in my childhood home in Longmeadow, sprung from our—mine, my brother's, the Two Sides of My Mothers'—collaged mourning.

Or, he was *never* born—he'd simply always been there, in my mind, a Memory available for hire and waiting, right off the page, for his moment.

I have to admit: In some ways I'd been preparing for the loss of my father my whole life. I'd expected it to break me and it did—the bile of loss scorched every surface inside me, incinerating some wires and parts completely and forcing others into new places in my body. I changed for good. I'd been a student—the Promise of a Book—and I became nothing: a poor father, a stumbling reporter, a really terrible lover. All the hair moved off my head and my stomach swelled with what I could not get back, with the terrible space of his no-voice, our non-talks, the never-again feeling of connecting with someone, of feeling understood, of being loved. I literally went to a new place in my own mind—drove off from some things and never returned to them. I built an entire world—OK, a county or two, but still—inside myself based on loneliness and bewilderment, on what was not, on the sounds things make when they crack, break, split, shatter, pop.

118

The Dogs didn't help things, either. I expected a massive search or news about suspects, but I didn't hear a bark from them. In the first month or so after the attack, I went to the Amherst CityDog Barracks twice a week and spoke through the window to the Dog on duty.

"Nothing new," he'd say as soon as I approached the glass.

"Are they still going out?" I'd ask. "Are they looking?"

He'd always tell me they were.

Finally I met with the Captain—sat in the leather chair in his office, looked him in the eye. He leaned over the desk, his paws crossed.

"We go out on tree patrols every day," the Captain said. "But truthfully, we have no leads on your tree at all."

"Did you try Montague?" I asked.

"Of course, but—"

"Charlemont?"

"It's not that simple," he said.

"Greenfield?"

"Mr. _____—it's not that we can't find Heart-Breed trees. But it's almost impossible to find one particular tree—not a Memory, mind you, but the tree itself!—if he wants to hide. Hell, this is why we try and get them to register!"

"How hard can it be to find a tree driving a farm?"

"These things survive by hiding, by camouflaging themselves. He could literally be anywhere—alive or dead, right under our nose or a thousand miles away."

"Isn't there anything you can do?" I said. "My *Dad*'s in that farm."

The Dog leaned back in his chair and pursed his lips. "Did you read the report? That hard-to-see Truck saw the whole thing."

I knew what he was implying. "Still," I said. "He could still be—"

"He's not," the Dog said. "Read what the Truck said about your Dad's *chest*."

It wasn't too long after that meeting—after the sentence of loss had begun to set itself in my mind and its rhythms became known to me—that I walked out the front door of the Crescent Street apartments, on my way somewhere, and noticed the Memory of My Father—a flickering image of my father at about fifty-five—balancing on some rickety scaffolding, doing something to the shakes or the gutter. I guess my mind had started to accept the version that my father was gone, that he wasn't ever coming back. At the time, in fact, his Memory wasn't even a surprise—I think I'd been building him my whole life, and to be honest I'm not even sure that this was the first time I noticed him. We had no formal introduction or conversation about our relationship, not even a hello. The Memory of My Father saw me staring up at his work and he climbed down to talk to me as if we'd seen each other five minutes earlier.

"I can't save it," he said. He was dressed in paint-covered jeans that once belonged to me, a too-tight flannel shirt from the Salvation Army and moccasin shoes that likely came from a tag sale. He looked out from behind tinted glasses in brown plastic frames.

"Save what?" I asked.

"The sophet," he said, looking up at the gutters. "It's all cracked to shit."

"Can't you just replace a section of it?"

He frowned, shook his head. "Whole fucking thing needs to go," he said.

"Shit," I said. "We're talking a good few hours, right?"

He cleared his throat and spit. "At least."

The more I lived with this Memory, the more I learned about its limitations—what it could and couldn't do. Sometimes it froze on me, and other times it did nothing but mimic my actions. I'd be powering at my desk, say, and when I picked up a stapler it would reach down and pick up the Memory of a Stapler. I'd type the words "How to Keep Your Volkswagen Alive," and it'd type "The Memory of How to Keep Your Volkswagen Alive."

There were also moments, though, when the Memory was a mystery, an evocation from a deep, hidden section of my mind. Not long after I saw him on the scaffolding, for example, I drove the VW home to my parents' house in Longmeadow and I saw the Memory of My Father again. This time he was painting the house a new color, a color called

Fear of Death. Apparently he'd decided to do this without asking anyone (which is just like my father!), not even the Two Sides of My Mother. Not that they would have objected—they spent their days now dressed in black, smoking their fingers in unison and staring out the window, as if by doing so they could change the course of trees and hearts.

The Memory of My Father saw the VW and I pull in and held up his hand. "Give me just a *second*, I'm almost done," he said, running his brush against the side of the house, then stepping back. He held out his arms. "What do you think?"

The color was so bright it almost hurt to look at. "It's not subtle," I said.

"You don't like it either? What the fuck! Everyone's been giving me shit about it."

"I didn't say I didn't like it. It's just—sort of loud."

"It'll fade, it'll fade!" he said. He was still holding the brush in his hand, and the Fear of Death rushed to the edge of the bristles and threatened to slip off and drop to the pavement.

"Won't that take years?" I said.

"Not with the weather we've been having."

I knew exactly what he was saying. "The inner weather, you mean?"

He put his hands on his waist. "What?" he said.

Later, the four of us—myself, the Memory of My Father and the Two Sides of My Mother—went out to Bridge's for pizza. Bridge's had been one of my parents' favorite places when my Dad was alive—the pizza there was brief and kind—and it felt good to be back there. And it was just like my father for the Memory of My Father to reach for the tab with his paint-stained hands and pay. This was symbolic, of course, because he didn't really know time, nor could he make it or lose it. He was, at that moment, my Dad back in the mid-1990s, when my father was renovating the Crescent Street apartments and pouring all that he had into them. My Dad's hair at the time was wild and gray, his glasses were gold-rimmed and his wallet, when you opened it, had nothing but sand inside.

It was during dinner that night, I think, that I more fully realized how this Memory worked—that it could change according to where I was in my mind, and that it was able to do certain things (work, pay) and not others (hug, sip tea, read or write). The Memory of My Father could say certain words or phrases, but others were hidden from him. Sometimes his image was almost completely transparent and other times it appeared so solid that you might actually think he was a real man.

When we came home that night we got a fresh glimpse of the Fear of Death, still tacky in the half-light. The color made the house look tragic, like carry-on luggage. House = luggage, flight = cavity/chest.

Plus, that evening the neighbors started calling about the color, and a few even knocked on our door. One man, a neighbor we'd never met before, had hair of solid gold. He stood in the doorway and said, "Tell me that's a primer."

I'd thought the Memory of My Father would have sworn at him, but by this point he was my father a few years later, and he was calmer and more content. "No," he said. "That's actually the color."

"What color is it?"

"It's called Fear of Death."

The neighbor crossed his arms, sighed and looked again at the front of the house. "*Boy*," he said. "I mean, it completely changes the neighborhood."

The Memory of My Father didn't say anything.

The man looked at him and said, "You're staring at my hair."

"No—no," the Memory of My Father said.

"You are."

My father even older now, the Memory of My Father flickered shyly and held up his hand. "Sorry, hey. I mean," he said.

"It's extremely heavy, in case you wondered," the man said.

"I can imagine."

"I constantly look for places where I can rest it."

"Well here," the Memory of My Father said. He held out his hands and the man put his gold head in them.

As the light faced the firing squad the Memory of My Father and I sat outside on the back patio, sipping the Memory of Beer. The Memory of My Father winced and custom-swore when he cracked the can, just like my father used to.

We both took deep sips as we looked at the color in the dark. Even lightless you could see its images.

After a moment the Memory of My Father asked, "Is it that bad?"

I reached into the swamp of my heart. "Course not," I said. "It's *true*. Who cares if it has meaning and weight?"

"I didn't mean to offend anyone with it," said the Memory of My Father, now my father as an old man—just weeks before the attack. "I just picked up the brush. It did all the talking."

"I know the name of *that* tune," I told him, and we both took a slug.

We sat there for a while more. Then the Memory of My Father fell asleep in the metal chair, and the chair wrapped its arms around him and held him there. I watched them lie together for a few minutes and then I put down my beer, stood up, went over to the side of the house and put my hands to the paint.

It was still alive—not yet dry, not yet dead. I touched it and it touched me back. All at once I knew Memories I'd forgotten, images that had made me. I felt an incubator. I knew the warm breath of my first refrigerator, the smell of the yellow kitchen floor. The first sign of an old soldier I never knew, his beard a forest of dying snow.

JAWS

If the quiet, teethy taupe of your VW's dashboard legumes, the VW is asking for **Jaws**—the Jaws Junkyard, on Route 66 in Westhampton. There are several junkyards in western Massachusetts—Highway Auto, Ludlow Salvage—but I know of no other yard as volkstocked as Jaws. They literally have *rows* of VW corpses to pick through. Also, they have a car in the front yard that was once a shark. I'm serious; it has fins and teeth but it drives on the road. I've never seen anything else quite like it.

I think of Jaws now and my lungs ache. How many afternoons, pre-attack, did I spend there with my father, picking through bodies for parts for our cars?

What I'm saying is, they have great prices.

If you do go to Jaws, though, remember that not all Volkswagens are the same. Some have external feeders, others have internal ones and some burn paperless altogether. I once lifted up an engine compartment lid on a VW at Jaws and found a nest of screaming birds. I opened another and found a field of crops. Where were the morning cables—the combustion chambers? I have no idea how it could be that the inside of each was so different, but there it was, for our review, the VW undercover variation.

Even so, always be sure that the part they give you is right for your car—the balloons at Jaws'll sell you any old part they can.

One time, the VW and I went out to Jaws to see about getting a new **believer**—the circuit which connects the storypump via sunrise to the middle transmission. In the weeks before that, the VW had stopped believing in almost everything—the road, the book of power, every story I told him. That's how I knew his believer was shot.

So I did what I had done so many times before—I drove us out to Westhampton, parked the VW at the salvage yard entrance and stepped into the office trailer. I spoke to a dirty red balloon who was sitting behind the counter, reading a magazine and eating a grinder.* When I leaned against the desk I could hear the stories in his chest—one about volume, another about a new set of curtains. He looked up at me and I said, "Looking for a new believer for my son."

The balloon put down his food and swiped his hands together. Then he picked up a clipboard. "What year is your son's car?"

"He *is* the car."

"What year?"

"Seventy-one," I said. "Beetle."

The balloon flipped a page on the clipboard. "Only one we have is a four-point from a state prison."

"A *prison*," I said.

---

* In Massachusetts, the word for a hoagie or sub sandwich.

The balloon nodded. "It should work. Beliefs for Bugs and state prisons—" he scanned the page—"should be interchangeable."

"You sure?"

"That's what the listing says."

"You don't have any VW believers—factory parts?"

The balloon let out a little air. "This is the only believer that I have on the whole lot," he said.

"How much?"

"Three and a half," he said.

"Could you order a Volkswagen-type believer from another yard?"

"I can put your name on a list," he said. "You need it right now?"

I looked out the window of the trailer and saw the VW studying a puddle of mud and antifreeze.

"I really do," I confessed. "Poor kid doesn't know *what* to believe."

• • •

From the moment the balloon handed me that dead, grey part (which, incidentally, was about the size and shape of a **bagel**), though, I should have known that it wasn't going to fit. But like a reese I bought it, took it home and tried to install it. When I removed the old believer, I found that it had *five* points—not four, like the prisoner. Nevertheless, I installed the new one and hoped for the best.

I knew immediately that it was a mistake. Shortly after the transaction, the VW asked me what time "chow" would be served. Later that night, he asked me about getting a tattoo.

For two days, the VW believed he was a prison. Every other word was caged—he spoke about solitary confinements and inmate rehabilitation. One night at dinner the following week, I asked him what his plans were for the evening and he mentioned his hopes to review proposals for new community outreach programs.

That was it—I'd heard enough. I threw down my fork and knife. "In the morning I'm taking you back to Jaws," I said, "and we're going to get you a new believer."

125

"If we can put these inmates to work, Dad—"

"Enough," I said.

"—we can help them *and* help the community."

I went back to Jaws the next day and spoke to the same balloon. "It doesn't fit," I said. "The kid believes that he's a state prison." I handed him the old, rotten believer. "See how this one has five points? The one you gave me has four."

I could hear the balloon's stories churning as he studied the part. "Remind me where this goes on your car," he said.

"It connects one of the transmissions to the storypump," I said.

The balloon looked up at me and his face turned a corner. "The transmission—to the *what*?" he said.

VI. RED LIGHT ON!

BREAK IT DOWN

CONDITION

Breakdown.

TOOLS AND MATERIALS

- One young, faulty 1971 Volkswagen Beetle
- A good-to-go gertrude
- Questionboats, at least two or three
- One poor booker

WHERE & WHEN

- On the way to school
- By Cooper's Corner in Florence Center
- On South Street, by the Northampton-Easthampton Q
- En route to a Sunderlandian
- On Market Street, outside Joe's
- Outside the Pleasant Street Theater
- Voking up Gothic
- Driving past the Northampton Airport
- Prasking towards a story in Leverett
- On the Northampton-Amherst Rail Trail
- Everywhere! After only a few months on the road, the kid was breaking down everywhere.

PROCEDURE (I)

We were driving down 63 in Leverett when the VW slowed to a stop and

I got out. "What's the story?" I said.

"You tell me," said the VW, coughing and shaking his head. "A *syllabus*?"

In those days my writing was dischordant, every note flat. I said, "So what?"

"A syllabus is *not* a story."

"Well, it's all I can come up with right now," I said.

"But I can't run on it."

"You can if you scan it right," I said.

"It's just a list, Dad—there's no Procedure, even! It's just a bunch of cheap words—"

"These words work fine."

"Not for me they don't," said the VW.

I threw my hands. "What do you want me to do?"

"Write!"

"Right here?" I said. "On the side of the road?"

The VW blinked.

"It'll take *hours*," I said.

"I don't care how long it takes," the VW said.

I custom-swore, grabbed my power from the front seat and sat down on the curb. "You like to make my life difficult, don't you?"

"How hard is it to write fuel?" the VW said. "All I need is a freaking A-to-B. A character, something!"

I tried. I put my hands on the keys. After a minute or so I said, "I can't think of anything!"

"Start with a conflict, how about," the VW said.

"Like what?"

"A problem—any problem."

"Here's a problem—I want to go home, but my son won't move."

"Fine—start there, then!" the VW said.

PROCEDURE (II)

Then there was the time we were daytripping towards the Quabbin and the VW started complaining about being tired. "Can we stop and rest for a second?" he asked.

"We're almost there—let's stop when we get there, OK?"

"How about a quick nap?"

"We're like five miles away!"

A mile or two later, though, the VW stalled. "What's happening, kiddo?" I said.

The VW didn't answer me.

"Hey!" I said. I hit the breaks, steered us into the breakdown lane and got out of the car.

The kid was fast asleep.

PROCEDURE (III)

Just a few miles past the Café Evolution, veeping onto Elm, the VW shouted a custom-made and coasted to a stop. I said, "Ey—what's happening?"

He mumbled an answer.

"What?" I said.

He was speaking too quietly for me to hear him—all I heard was "wrong road."

I got out of the car and went around to the front. The VW was studying the pavement. "What's the problem?" I said.

"This is the wrong version," he said. "There's a history here."

"A what?"

"Listen." The VW put his ear to the asphalt. "There was a stadium right here—a huge baseball field with rows of seats. This is where Northampton's team, the Words and Pictures, used to play."

"It was?" I said.

"Right here! I was the shortstop."

I put my hands on my hips, suddenly realizing what was happening. "VW—"

"We were the best team in western Massachusetts. I remember ol' Glue Stevenson, who played third—"

"There wasn't ever a stadium here, kiddo," I said. "You're having problems with your memory coil is all."

"—was at the plate this one night, against a mean, cantered industrial grill—"

"This is all just a bad coil-wrap."

"And that grill had the best continue-pitch in the league."

"OK. You can tell me this story at home, alright?"

"You mean keep going? No way," said the VW.

"What? Why not?"

"Dad, this spot is *historical* for me. How can you expect me to just drive over the field's Memory as if it wasn't ever here?"

"Because it wasn't," I said.

"It was—you just don't remember it," the VW said.

"Can we please go home now?"

The VW shook his head. "I'm staying right here."

"You're kidding me," I said.

"I'm not kidding at all," the VW said.

And he wasn't. I pleaded with the VW to let the "memory" go, but he wouldn't move. I had to call a tow truck to get us both home.

PROCEDURE (IV)

The VW would start to lurch and sputter, and then he'd stop running altogether. I'd get out of the car and open the engine compartment. When I did I'd find:

- A landfill
- A candy store
- A factory of some sort
- I don't know, but something took my picture
- An old woman, pointing her finger at me and shaking her head

"What do you see?" the VW'd say.

I'd tell him.

"Can you fix it?" he'd ask.

Hardly ever!

"Of course I can," I'd say.

VALVE ADJUSTMENT

There was the half-faced woman and the Scientist, and then there was the Lady Made Entirely of Stained Glass, who lived and worked at the Don Muller Gallery in Northampton. I really came close to loving this woman; she was bright and creative, an artist, and I could spend a good deal of money with her without feeling the draw of the power. She was also the one who told me about the village of Shelburne Falls, incidentally, because she was born there—forged by a mother (raw sand) and a father (a glass-blowing factory film) out on the scene of the body of glacier-pockmarked stone called the Potholes.

I met the Lady Made Entirely of Stained Glass at the Paradise City Arts Festival, where she was selling handmade moods. Each one was completely unique, and it came with its own case and certificate of authenticity. I was supposed to be there to write a story for the *Wheel,* but as we were browsing the tables the VW became fascinated by one of these moods—a new sort of skepticism—and he wouldn't put it down.

"How did you get the happiness in there?" the VW asked the Lady Made Entirely of Stained Glass, who stood behind her table in a simple black dress.

"I work with a microscope," she explained. "I fused the happiness with a steady disbelief."

"Jeez. It must have taken so much *money,*" the VW said.

"It did—"

"It's *beautiful,*" the VW said. "It's a beautiful mood."

"Thanks, man," she said. "It's cool that you like it so much."

I didn't say anything. To be honest, I was intimidated by her beauty—by the way the light attached itself to her, passed through her multi-hued cheeks and neck and hair and sprang from it as if somehow stronger.

After a few minutes I told the VW to put the mood down. He begged me to buy it, but I said no. It wasn't even an option for me—I just didn't have the time with me.

"You know what?" the Lady Made Entirely of Stained Glass said. "This one's on the house. Take it."

The VW's eyes brightened. "Really?"

"No," I said to him. Then I turned to her. "That's very kind. But I can't let you—"

"I'm not giving it to you," she said to me. "I'm giving it to *him*."

"Yeah," the VW said. He put the mood on and his face became very suspicious.

"Take that off," I said to him. Then I turned back to her. "Really—"

"Too late—done deal," she said. "He digs it too much for him not to have it."

"Please," I said. "That's just too much. Can I at least give you something for it?" She continued to refuse, but as she did so I saw a very tiny wisp of interest in the glass housing behind her eyebrows. I had to stare at it for a few moments before I was even sure it was interest. But it was.

So I asked her if I could take her to dinner.

She held the question in her mind for a moment, and then looked into her hands. "You don't need to do that—it's not that big of a deal."

"Even so," I said. "Dinner."

"No," she said, clouding.

"I'll go too," the VW said.

She stared at me.

"Dinner," I said again.

The Lady Made Entirely of Stained Glass and I went on a few dates—to dinner, to a play that the VW had worked on as an understudy—and then things grew folk; she started spending nights at my place, or I went to hers. I met her mother-of-sand; she came with me when I met the Two Sides of My Mother for breakfast one morning.

We had a lot of faith in each other, and sometimes when we did there was enough light—from the candles, from the moon—for the Lady Made Entirely of Stained Glass's body to catch it, and then I could see myself inside her, see every aspect of that process, the soft and mysterious machine of her body as it moved against mine. It felt like a real relationship; the VW and I stopped going to the Castaway, even!

But these kind of stories—love stories, stories with faith—are apparently not the kind that I was built to book, either that or I haven't yet learned *how* to book them. As it turned out, the Lady Made Entirely of Stained Glass was too fragile for me; every time we argued or our discussion warmed, her body grew cold and brittle. If she wasn't careful, she told me, it could crack.

One night we had a very heated argument—she wanted me to move in with her, and I was reluctant to do so because I had to run the Crescent Street apartments—and we couldn't resolve it. We went to bed angry—she on her side of the bed, me on mine.

That night I dreamt I had all the time in Northampton.

I woke up next to a pile of broken stained glass, and my legs were all cut and pleading. I did all the screaming—the pile of glass was completely silent.

Had *I* done that? Had I destroyed the Lady Made Entirely of Stained Glass, because her glass was fragile and I rolled over in my sleep? Or had she been so cold that she shattered?

You see what I mean: The story fails, it has a heart attack, it needs something I can't give it.

I never did get rid of that stained glass, though. A year later, when the VW was really ill, one of his eyes shattered and I used some of the stained glass to repair it. Every time I drove at night from that point on, colors from the Lady Made Entirely of Stained Glass's skin—pinks, blues, greens—were broadcast onto the roads of Northampton.

Years and years later, though, after I'd left it all behind and moved away, I saw a woman who looked exactly like the Lady Made Entirely of Stained Glass. She was dressed in a blue uniform with an orange vest, standing in one of those wooden boxed platforms in the middle of a busy intersection, directing traffic outside a fair. I was so stunned when I saw her that I stepped out into the middle of the traffic and approached her.

She saw me and pointed. "Step back to the curb!" she yelled.

The cars coming towards me slowed down. I held up my hand. "It's me," I said.

She put her hands on her glass hips. "Sir, step back to the curb!" she said again.

I kept walking forward.

"Sir!" she bolted.

I smiled as I looked up at her. "I don't know if I did something wrong that night, or if I just wasn't able to tell the story right, or what," I said.

Now we stood in the center of the road and the traffic moved around us. Her look was a fist. "You have me confused with someone else, sir," she said. "Now, please—go back to the sidewalk."

"The Volkswagen?" I said. "Northampton, Massachusetts? Remember?"

Her glass hair shone from beneath her blue hat. "Sir, I'm trying to do my job—"

"It *is* you," I said.

Her arms were waving madly at the traffic. "I'm not the person you're looking for," she said.

But she was. I saw the Memory in her mind: my own image, the pink cloud of fear attached to it.

THE VOLKSWAGEN IS MUSIC II

Sometimes you can make the tune travel, even travel in it. I don't know if this happened in the town where you grew up (Did it? Type or speak your answer into the power—or just think it, and the book will catch the thought.), but it happens all the time in western Massachusetts. Like I've said, these mirkins were everywhere, cupping every aspect of our lives—the weather, our financial status, collective mood and travel conditions. They were in the walls of our homes, our books, our clothes, even! I once had a hell of a pair of musical pants, for example—the notes fit me just right. An ex-girlfriend borrowed them from me, though, and that was the last I saw of them.

In the Volkswagen, incidentally, stories and songs were the exact same thing. I've received several deets about this, zoffers coasting keys and rhythm. Dizzyspeak aside, though, I think it's clear that we're all always instrumenting—either versing and chorusing, or "His name was Sneaker" and "Later that night I called Edna and asked if we could meet"ing.

Whether you're esking, fisking or a little of both, though, the practice is only good for so much. Music'll get you to the store, and maybe from Northampton to Amherst. But can we reach people with it—really *reach* them? No. How many times, after my father's disappearance, did I send out songs for him? I can't even give you a number. For a while there I would leave work in the afternoons, find a place where I could dean— the campus of the old abandoned mental hospital, the Prayer Wheel at UMass—and try and build distance from those old country tunes we once shared. I yelled as loud and as strong as I could in every direction. But what good did it do me? Every tune I sent came back empty and cold. At the end of every story my father was still gone, still dead.

But what did I expect? Songs don't have *hearts*—they're just mindless vessels of notes and beats. This is why 90, 91 and other multitunes are so frightening—they're nothing but sheer force and character. Hell, most of the time you don't even hear a melody until you're in it—until you notice, after some money, that your surroundings have changed, that something has shifted. All of a sudden you look through the windshield and find yourself mid-chorus, or stopped inside a note or unresolved phrase.

There are positives and negatives with this kind of travel. Driving through music is exciting, first, because you can see things you'd never see on sidestreets: double-timed Veggienotes, racing codas, rests restocitating at sidestops on the shoulder. Plus, all money loses value—it must, by virtue of the fact that you're traveling through a specific measure at a speed unique to you and your vehicle. In many ways that's a good thing;

you can relax, there's no need to worry. It doesn't matter how fast or slow you drive; you'll get there when you get there!

For the very same reason, though, music is an inefficient way to travel. A big reason for this is the fact that notes/characters are finite—once they die, that is, you can't go back through them. If you've gone more than a few measures it's impossible to turn around. You have to see the story through, however long it takes. Plus, there are mistakes made all the time—tunes sent at random, or directed to one person and unknowingly read by another.

One time, for example, the VW and I were tracking a story for the *Wheel* when we picked up a storytune—a swooning dirge—that wasn't meant for us. The maul was sent by a woman whose mother had died just minutes before. She'd intended to target her husband, a long-haul truck about a half-mile behind us, but in her grief she'd picked us up instead.

The VW and I didn't know any of this at the time, of course—we picked up the song, realized we were on it, and followed it. After some time—it's hard to say how long—we arrived at the ledge of a window on a high floor of a hospital; the final chord twisted right up to the glass.

The poor woman drifted over and opened up the window. Her face was a spiral staircase. Her eyes attacked mine. "You're not Gary," she said.

"No," I said. I immediately understood what had happened. "I'm not." I looked past the woman at the window. There was a dead body—that of an old woman, nearly bald—in the hospital bed.

I quickly turned the VW around and we drove back the way we came, passing the truck on our way out. By now I'd almost certainly missed my assignment. Plus, this trip had left the VW low on stories and we had a long way to go before we made it back. So I had to power on the spot, which I hated.

We raced back through the song, knowing full well that the first plot points were probably dead. We were able to make it back through the fourth chorus and the third verse, but then we hit traffic—VeggieCars, bioleggers and Volkswagens as far as I could see. I tried to look past them—was that the end of the chapter up there?

As we slowed to a crawl I grew anxious—I was gripping the wheel with my hands and custom-swearing.

"Dad," the VW said. "What's the problem?"

"My *job* is the problem," I said. "I'm missing the story—who knows how much money is passing outside this tune?"

Soon we saw why the traffic was backed up: A VeggieCar had hit the edge of a note—trying, as we all were, to make it back. The car was crushed—there were bits of VeggieEngine all over the place—and two CityDogs were loading an older woman on a stretcher into an ambulance.

Past the crushed car was another CityDog, diverting traffic onto a detour tune—one set up to get the stranded passengers back to western Massachusetts via a different premise. We followed the detour until we could see the definite break in the sky where the fluorescent song ended and the looming Route 9 began again.

I didn't get back to the *Wheel* until about four in the afternoon. When I walked into the office I saw Louise, standing at my desk with her arms crossed. "Where the *hell* have you been?" she cheesed.

"Wrong story," I said. "We got lost."

"For two weeks?" she said.

I held my hands out to her. "There was an accident," I said.

RED LIGHT ON!

PROCEDURE

You have come to this chapter because the red light on the dashboard is burning—because the VW is asking for something and you need to know what. The red light is the **Castaway Light**; if it goes on, it's time to get onto Route 5 and head out to Whately. You'll know you're close when you see a field of Troubadourians grazing in a field to your right and the

Antiquarian on your left. Then the road will whistle low. About a mile down the road, you'll see the pink and white moor of the Castaway.

The VW loved so many places in western Massachusetts—the Prayer Wheel, the Mill, the Moan—but none so much as the Castaway. This wasn't just a fun cove to undrive; it played an essential role in the overall motion for my son, in the connecting of one thread to another. I suspect the same is true for your car. Do you see, behind the wrap of Northampton, the tune-souled road that runs by two bookstores? Follow that road until you see the sequined coils of the Castaway. You can't miss it!

Inside the Castaway, you'll find men and women drinking the Promise of Beer at small, wooden tables while watching the ideas take off their clothes. I've seen an oven take off its bikini slow, a cactus saunter through the tables in a mini-skirt and tube top, the Memory of a hanged slave throw his overalls into the crowd.

You can see, as you sit at the bar, that the Castaway is not only about faith—though plenty of faith occurs—but also about *revision*, about moving from one draft of the Volkswagen to the next. Each of us has several skins. Say we could have found the time to sit at the bar together, you and I. And let's say we saw one of the Castaway regulars—the toaster, say—step up on stage and take off her clothes, as she does at least once a week. She strips to encourage faith—a *reader's* faith—but also to be free. You would see that underneath her clothes, the toaster is a wooded backyard in the moonlight. You see? It's neither the sweet music nor the driving beer that prompts the Castaway; it's the fact that an overworked toaster can unplug from the wall, lift her shirt and reveal a thicket of trees.

Drink enough Memories of Beer, though, and everything will quiet down for you. Then you'll hear it—that **one note** inside your chest that you know is real, the one that no one can buy, steal or retune.

THE STORY

There are many wires that head back to the Castaway, but this one, which takes place much later—in 2005, actually—is certainly the thickest and most traveled.

Inside the Castaway that night, the air was rich with narrative and all of the stories were saying the same thing. The posters on the wall yelled insults to one another while a group of instruments set themselves up in the corner and two white plastic cups danced on stage.

It's worth pointing out, incidentally, that everyone I've ever taken to the Castaway—my brother, my son, the Chest—has managed at one point or another to secure themselves at least a little bit of faith there. But not me. Every time I tried—sitting down next to a lonely airport lounge and trying to heat up a conversation; suggesting to a stereo that we take a walk outside—it turned sour. I believed and they didn't. There was something about me—either I wasn't attractive enough, or I lacked confidence, or they could see something in me that I myself couldn't see.

That night, my son went to sit by the stage with a MemoryBeer and I tried to find a seat at the bar. In a few minutes one opened up and I sat down and ordered the darkest Memory on the wall. As I drank it, I looked around at the people huddled on the stools; almost every one of them was a no-face or misface, men and women for whom things had gone wrong.

The VW, meanwhile, went to sit by the stage, and soon enough he'd started laughing and drinking with a Kandinsky Print—a regular image at the Castaway. She was chatting casually with him, her feet on the chair and a drink in her hand, but her composition twinkled in a way that told me she had something more in mind. I predicted that the two of them would soon disappear.

Then I stopped paying attention to the VW, though, because I began talking with an old vice—she'd asked me about the Volkswagen and I started telling her stories. I told her about his health, how he was sick all the time, and then about his mother, how she'd left me to raise the VW by myself. I suppose I mentioned this so the vice would have pity on me, and maybe generate a little faith for me, but when I mentioned the Lady from the Land of the Beans the vice slapped the bar with her hand.

"You're kidding me," she said. "She doesn't help at all?"

"She's hundreds of miles away!" I said.

Her face was gritty, scratched. "How can she not want any involvement in her son's life?"

"Well, the VW *is* in touch with her—they do speak about once a week on the phone."

The vice was quiet as she registered this. Then she said, "Oh."

"And he spent a week last summer with her in the Land of the Beans."

"He did?" the vice asked.

"Sure."

"Well why didn't you tell me that?"

"I just did."

"I mean before, when you were telling me all of those stories?"

I put my drink down—I was a little dizzy, too beered up for this conversation. "My point is—"

"The woman didn't abandon him—it sounds like she does what she can." The vice pointed to my power. "How many stories does that thing hold?"

"A lot—at least fifty," I boasted.

"Are there stories about her in there?"

"Some," I said defensively.

"About her role in the VW's life?"

I looked down at the tangle of tape and dust.

"See?" she said.

"That doesn't mean anything," I said. "You're making a big deal out of nothing."

"It's *not* nothing—I'm listening to what you're saying, and I'm trusting you to be fair."

"*Fair?*" I said. "Who said anything about being fair?"

And that's when the VW tapped me on the shoulder. "*Dad,*" he hissed.

I turned to face him.

"Did you see that tree over there? The one with the note-coat?"

"Where?"

"Across the bar," he said.

I looked.

The tree was sitting on a stool, drinking a beer. He had a moustache and a baseball hat. His vest was harmonizing with the music from the jukebox, but upon first glance he didn't look to be any different from the firs and cherries that sometimes stumble-twigged into the bar.

I said, "I'm in the middle of a conversation, OK buddy?"

"But—"

"I thought you were chatting with the Kandinsky Print."

"Dad—" the VW gasped.

"—we can't get excited every time we see a tree, kiddo."

"But *that* tree has blood on his chin," the VW said.

Did he? I looked again. "No he doesn't," I said.

"Yes, he does," the VW said.

"You've probably just had too much to drink."

"I have not," the VW said. "I'm telling you—"

"Go back to the print," I said.

I went back to my conversation with the vice—I was still hoping that something might develop. A few minutes later, though, I saw the tree stand up and pay his time. Then he turned on his tree-heels, pushed open the door and walked out into the night.

The VW sped across the room and followed him out. Before I knew what was happening I was walking out too.

By the time I reached the dusty parking lot, the VW was standing in the middle of Route 5. "Dad—look!" he said, pointing north.

The whole *night* was ringing—the stars, the homes, the road itself.

I looked. All I saw was a yellow light in the distance.

"Isn't that a farm?"

I looked again. Was that light in the shape of a *window*? No. "I don't think so—it's a shed or something."

"It might not be," the VW said. "Come on—let's follow it. It might be a pasture."

"It's *not* a pasture."

"I think it is," the VW said.

"We can't, VW," I said. "*You* can't."

"I'm fine!"

"Let's go home, alright?"

The VW shot me a ditto-face. "Dad," the VW said. "Don't you hear the music?"

And I did—I did hear music. But so what? I said, "We've both had too much MemoryBeer, is all."

"I'm telling you, that tree was—"

"No it wasn't."

The VW threw down his hands. "I can't believe you! Why can't we—"

"Because I said no, OK? No."

The VW shook his head in disgust. "You're making a mistake," he said.

"It wouldn't be the first time," I admitted.

The VW turned to face south, towards home. I got in and we started driving through the dark. After a moment the VW said, "You know what, Dad?"

"What?" I said.

"When I get older? I won't be like you."

"Oh really?" I said.

"That's right. I won't watch my whole life, every opportunity I'm given, go the other way."

I was offended, then angry. I said, "VW, you *are* older."

"I am not," he said. "I've got my whole life ahead of me. My *real* life hasn't even really begun."

I shook my head. "That's not true. You're a nineteen seventy-one Volkswagen Beetle—a thirty-five year old car. You're older than *I* am, for god's sake."

The VW seemed to mull this over for a second, as we vaulted through Hatfield and towards the Northampton line. Then he said, "You're just trying to hurt my feelings. I'm not even three freaking years old."

"It's too late for you, VW, just like it's too late for me," I said.

"I don't believe you," the VW said. "I'm still fresh and new, with only a few dents on me, and I'm going to grow up to be a—"

"VW," I said, "You're already everything you're ever going to be."

Later on, I came back to Northampton with the woman I was dating—a Scientist, who worked with infectious diseases—and we went down to the store called Faces to see about getting my name back. This was years in the future—my father was dead and the Crescent Street house just a Memory. When the Scientist and I turned onto Main Street we found it completely changed: Most of the stores had died and were just stiff corpses on the sidewalk, their doors swinging open to expose ribs and grey lungs. And the only cars on the road anymore were VeggieCars— rows of half-rotten jalopies lining either side of Main Street.

The Scientist and I had a complex relationship, which is to say that sometimes she was fond of me and other times she treated me like an orange traffic cone. She'd been nice enough to me to take me in after I'd lost my father's house, but sometimes she gave me a look that meant I was to go away, to leave for several days.

It was then that I called the Memory of the Volkswagen, who barely spoke to me otherwise.

"What," he'd say when he answered the phone.

Other times, the Scientist would let me stay out of pity, but under a particular arrangement: I slept in her living room or on the kitchen floor, priming in a sleeping bag, while she went out to the chemi-clubs to find young men and women. I would lie awake, listening to them faithing in the next room, moaning and lying.

But something kept us together, at least for a time. She was honest and jaw, and I was soft and afraid, and maybe she liked the fact that I would do whatever she told me to. I was happy to oblige in any way I could, even if that meant leaving or curling up to the refrigerator for warmth while she cried out in faith in the bedroom.

Once every few weeks or so, though, the Scientist would open her bed to me and I would climb in, and she would float above me, sus- pended, and touch me *here*, and *here* and *here*. As she did, I could feel myself getting infected with whatever condition or virus she was carrying at the moment. This explained the pain in my groin. Sometimes I had trouble urinating. For a few weeks I lost all track of time.

But by that time I didn't even really mind. I was old, and without knowing it I had carved out spaces in my life for each of these conditions. In some subconscious way, I think I wanted them.

That morning, we stood at the counter in Faces until a teenager came to the register. She had lightattoos all over her and her head was completely sized.

I told her that I was there to buy back a name which I had sold to the store years earlier. She punched some keys on the back of a transaction animal—a dog-like creature bred and modified for retail—who sat patiently on the glass countertop, staring at me blankly.

"So," the girl said. "This was a name you leased to us?"

"I sold it," I said. "I needed the time for a constant velocity joint for—"

"Sold it *when*?" The girl's eyes were gutters.

"Fall, two thousand and three," I told her.

The girl scrunched up her face. "We usually don't keep our names for more than four years, even if they don't sell," she said. "They go out of style, see?"

"Can you just check for us?" the Scientist said, and she slid her arm around my waist. Her face was lumpy, soft.

The girl typed data into the buttons on the back of the animal. "Hm," she said, reading the backscreen. "City Life?"

I shook my head. "I had a small child at the time, a Volkswagen?" I said.

"What's a voke wagon?" the girl asked.

I was getting irritated. "Volkswagen. It was a type of car," I explained. "He was about—" I tried to think back, "two, two and a half. He was very sick. I needed some quick time, and I'd already sold every moment I could spare."

"Well, I'm not seeing any other names bought in two thousand three," she said. "Do you *remember* the name—what it sounded like?"

"I don't," I said.

The girl spoke into her wristmike and asked for a manager, and a minute later one appeared. He looked to be about twenty, and I noticed that his ears had been altered; he'd had small black speakers installed in his eardrums. "Here I am," he sang to her. "Hi," he said to us.

I nodded.

"They're trying to buy back a name that they sold us ten years ago," the girl said.

"Not quite that long," I said. "Two thousand three."

"Hm," the man said. "We don't usually ... what was the name?"

I winced.

"We're not sure," the Scientist explained.

"You don't remember the name?" he said.

"I don't. I just remember that it was fall, two thousand three, and that I had my son with me. He was ill that day and he spit up all over the carpets."

The manager wasn't really listening to me—he was searching through the database on the backscreen. As he did, the transaction animal shifted in place and itched under his arm, never taking his eyes off of me. These animals frightened me—I had seen footage of them chasing shoplifters down the street, their metal teeth glinting, their bellies bouncing with time.

After another minute the manager shook his head and looked up at me. "I'm not seeing it here," he said.

"That's what I told them," said the girl.

"What does that mean?" I said.

"See, we're not really in the business of selling names or faces back to their original owners," he said. "Sometimes, if someone comes in looking to buy back their name and they remember the features, we might still have it or have records of who we sold it to. But that's pretty rare."

I leaned on the glass counter, which featured a few of the store's most expensive faces. "I've saved up a lot of time to buy this name back," I said.

"What if we show you another name?" the manager said.

"I don't *want* another name—I want mine."

A line of people had started to form behind us. "Honey," the Scientist said.

"I'm really very sorry," said the manager.

"It was long—it was long!" I said. "Four names, strung together."

The man pressed his lips together. "That's not really enough for us to go on," he said.

I dug my fist against the top of the glass case and the faces beneath it rattled. The transaction animal bristled and showed its teeth. "I have the *time* now," I said. "I'll give you as much as you want."

The manager didn't say anything. The look on his face was the yellow lines of Route 47—both had the same hatch marks, the same pattern of wear.

The Scientist excused us and led me outside onto the sidewalk. "It's just a name," she said.

The sky was naked and far too wide. "The Other Side of My Mother gave me that name," I told her.

"Then how can you not remember it? How is that possible?"

"I don't know," I yelled into the morning. "But I don't."

She took my hands. "Think back," she said.

"Please," I huffered. "Don't try to tell me how to navigate my own memory. It's like a junkfarm in there, alright? Everything is rotted and picked through."

She let go of my hands. "Alright."

"It's a graveyard," I said, "filled with the dead and the decomposed."

"*OK*," she whispered. She started walking. "Enough, alright? Can we just go home?"

"This is what I've been saying to you," I said, following her down the sidewalk. "How am I supposed to communicate—to tell you how I feel—if all I have are the *bones* of words?"

LEAVES OF GRASS

A few weeks after we saw that vested tree at the Castaway, Goshen

CityDogs picked up a hospital hitchhiking along Route 9. When they found him he was without words, completely storyless—just a shut-down, abandoned emergency room in critical condition.

The Dogs rushed the hospital to Holyoke Hospital and they fed him stories intravenously. From what I was told, he very well might have died. Four or five days after his arrival, though, his backup generators kicked on and he started talking. The Dogs bedogged him, and when he mentioned Atkin's Farm they called me. The VW and I drove down to Holyoke and two Dogs met us at the main entrance.

"He's shown remarkable improvements," said a SergeantDog, leading me and my son into the elevator. "But I should warn you that he can't really speak yet."

"He can't speak?" the VW said.

"He hasn't gotten his voice back," the second Dog told us.

"We've been communicating to him through writing, mostly," said the Sergeant.

The elevator wrapped its arms around us and we were lifted.

"Has he said anything about my father?"

The Sergeant shook his head. "He's barely awake," he said. "At first we just thought that he was a drifter, a hitcher traveling down from Ash-field or something. Yesterday, he jotted down the initials 'AF.' Robert here suggested that it might mean Atkin's Farm, and we started to put blues and greens together."

The elevator released us and we were led past a guard Dog and into the hospital's hospital room, where I saw a gaunt, ghost-white building with storytubes and morning cables attached to his roof and every window. He was hardly even a Memory of the starched, orderlied Cooley-Dickinson that I remember.

The Sergeant leaned over the bed. "Mr. Dickinson?" he said.

The hospital opened his eyes. When he saw me, he raised a frail hallway and pointed it at me.

"Mr. Dickinson, this is—"

But the hospital dropped the hallway, closed his eyes and fell asleep.

・・・

While we sat in the waiting room the VW pressed me to speculate. "He *must* know where the Tree is, right?"

I shrugged.

"And the farm?"

"I don't know, kiddo," I said.

"When he tells me where that fucking Heart Attacker is—"

"Whoa—take it easy."

"I'm going to track him down and kick his *ass.*"

"No you are *not,*" I said.

"I am—I am," he said. As he spoke, I saw that the VW was shivering. "I'm going to make him *pay*—"

"VW—are you cold?"

"No," he umped.

"You're shivering."

"I am not."

"Kiddo, I can see—"

"I'm fine, Dad!"

Then the second Dog stuck his nose into the waiting room. "He's awake," he said.

We walked down the hall and into the hospital's room. The Sergeant-Dog nodded at me. "Mr. Dickinson," he said, "this is—"

The hospital mouthed a phrase I couldn't catch.

"I'm sorry?" said the Sergeant.

"_____," the hospital gasped.

"Yes," the Sergeant said. "_____, and his son, the nineteen seventy-one Volkswagen Beetle."

"I met you once before," I speckled. "Your surgery saved me, actually. You might not remember—"

"Mr. Dickinson," the Sergeant said, "we brought _____ here because his father was thought to have been with you when the tree—"

The hospital nodded and gestured towards the pencil and pad on the table next to the bed, and the second Dog reached for it. The hospital took the pad in his cement hands and wrote something down. Then he turned to show us. The pad read:

find him!

"Find him?" I said.

"Find who?" the VW said.

The hospital wrote, *sent songs.*

"Find the Tree?" I said.

"Mr. Dickinson," said the Sergeant, "where is the Tree now?"

The hospital wrote, *WAS alive.*

"The Tree was alive?" I said.

"Or my grandfather?" the VW said. "Was my *grandfather* alive?"

The hospital pointed to the VW, then wrote, *WAS. now ?*

tree fed stories. we all dd, tried.

"The Heart Attack Tree fed *my father* stories?"

The hospital nodded and scratched madly into the pad. *apple stories, pastry stories, pasture narativs.*

but NOW—no more stories, anywhere on the farm. why I ran away! dying.

"Mr. Dickinson, where is the Tree now?" the Sergeant Dog repeated.

have to FIND THEM

"But where?" the VW asked. "Where are they?"

The hospital closed his eyes, let the pad fall onto his chest and lay still for a minute or two. We all stared at him. For a moment I thought he'd fallen asleep again. Then he opened his eyes and picked up the pad. He wrote, *here!*

"Here *where?*" I said.

noho, florence. whatly hatfield. right here!

"This morning he told us that the Tree had been hiding the farm at Northampton-area trailer parks, dead-end streets and abandoned wooded areas," the Sergeant said. "We're checking those now."

laying lo, stealing hearts

"Are you kidding me?" the VW said. "He's been this fucking close the whole time?"

"VW—language! What did I say about that word?"

last I heard, went west. thru Greenfld? to S—F?

"What's SF?" the second Dog asked.

I thought about it. "Shelburne Falls?"

The hospital pointed at me. Then he wrote, *Tr. parkd farm outside grocery story—ran in for some milk.*

I tk my chance, ran for it.

The VW turned to me. "We're going there—right Dad? We're going after him."

"No we aren't," I said.

The SergeantDog extended his paws. "Let's take one step at a time here," he said.

The hospital started writing furiously.

"The first thing is get you healthy," the Sergeant told the hospital. "Then we'll resume our search for the farm."

The hospital threw the pad down and pointed at me. His eyes met mine. "*Your dad is sitting there—waiting for you,*" he gasped. "*He—needs stories.*"

"I realize that," I said. "But I just can't—"

"Now!" said the hospital. His voice was faint and hoarse, but his eyes were bullets. "Before it's too late!"

VII. ENGINE STOPS OR WON'T START

RAP ON OIL

If the green light on your VW's dash goes on, it's time to change your car's **sufferoil**. Sufferoil licks the engine of the Volkswagen and collects in a **sufferpan** underneath the engine at the rear of the car. Sometimes the gasket that connects the sufferpan to the rest of the car can split or leak, and then it's necessary to change that entire gasket, or perhaps even the pan itself. Otherwise, though, changing the sufferoil is a simple Q and A. Q: The oil and the filter? A: Yes!

And while it *is* simple, it's also incredibly important. The sufferoil holds those moments in the VW's experiences that are too cold, bright or sharp. These experiences turn over and over in the Volkswagen's muscles and limbs if you don't regularly change the oil and clean them out. Is your Volkswagen depressed? Is he or she driving slower and more sluggish than usual, or crying at the storypump? Maybe he or she is carrying around some heavy western masses—a death, a bad interaction with a tractor trailer, maybe even the sight of roadkill or a family of lost, hungry soda cans wandering down the side of Route 5 near the center of Greenfield. Whatever the case, it's your job as a parent to remove these moments and sketches before they seep into the memory coil and become fixed. There are experiences to <u>hold onto</u>, but you must <u>let go</u> of others or else they'll damage your VW permanently. Therefore, change your car's oil every fifty pages. Take out all of those heavy words, drop the storyfilter and change out any moments that are overly-sad or lonely. Let him or her feel new again. I've taken out whole characters (the Lady from the Land of the Beans), cut complete narratives short because they felt sluggish and mean, and you'd be amazed at how much lighter and faster my son could move after such changes.

Here's a stepper for how to do it:

Step 1. Use a non-emotional wrench to loosen and remove the six **sufferbolts** located in the bottom center of the car. As their name suggests, these bolts may have wars in their bellies and may therefore be tough to turn. This is why it's so essential that you use a confident, no-bullshit wrench; if a look-away gets ahold of these coats, and either smells the suffering in the gasket or talks about it with the bolts, the wrench is liable to give up or feign a great struggle. Remember that these bolts already have enough to worry about, as they're the keeper of secret, pressure-filled narratives, stories with depression turns and lost acres, burdens in their own right.

Step 2. Once you've removed the plugs, let the oil drain into a pan. Be aware: This oil is dangerous stuff, as it not only holds a local history of suffering—a collage of moments experienced by the Volkswagen and those who have ridden in him (this means *you*), and all those he's come into contact with since his last oil change—but also select moments of common suffering: hungry children farming VeggieCar fields, graves filled with murdered sneakers, mandolins clawing at the windows of moustached, sour-faced trains, Conceivable Beards sad in their graves. This is another reason to change the oil frequently (and thus, flush those tales out of the Volkswagen), and *to avoid getting any of this oil—any of these stories—on your hands.* Once my hand slipped while I was draining the sufferoil in my Volkswagen, and I was infected with the story of a Smith College student who drowned herself in a public fountain. It took twenty-four hours for that story to clear from my blood, and those hours were some of the most difficult I'd ever encountered—every word was a prison, every note the same.

Note, too, your Volkswagen's limits—that sometimes he or she can't discern between *real life* and *stories*, what is on one side of the windshield and what is on the other. This confusion is especially common when his oil has thickened with living to the point that it can't pass through the pre-Memory filter. This filter can be changed, but it's hartford to get to. It's best, then, to keep on top of the sufferoil situation and avoid putting yourself in this predicament.

As you pour the oil into the pan, you'll see and hear the suffering—it will play for you in warped liquid images and call out in twisted, muffled sounds. My advice, then, is to avoid looking at it whenever possible. If not, you might be reminded of something terrible and senseless, or see yourself or someone that you love in situations that will hurt to relive. During the first year that I had my Volkswagen, for example, I made the mistake of studying an image in the oil and I realized that it was *me*, on the operating table at twelve, the doctors' hands on me, the life of the Volkswagen at stake. Another time I saw Old Forever, shuffling into the bathroom late one morning, his mind a thicket.

Step 3. Once you pour the oil into the pan, bring it to the Northampton Waste Center where they'll bury it in lined canisters. *Don't* leave the oil around the house. I know a smooth who poured old sufferoil in a five-gallon bucket and left it in his garage, and his own experiences leaked out of the bucket and seeped into the pavement, the sewage system, the yard and finally into the foundation of his house. Years later he was still finding burgundies shivering in his kitchen cabinets, scurrying when he turned on the lights.

The oil, when you pour it, will start to scream. It knows about time and is frightened. And it should be—its life as we know it is over. No one knows what happens, or will happen, with the oil that we've buried. But the best thing you can do here is change the oil quick, avoid contact with it and get rid of it immediately.

NEVER put old oil back into the car, even in an emergency. You'll wind up with rescreens and morphs, situations you know stocked with odd hybrid characters. There is no faster way to sadden or confuse your Volkswagen beyond repair.

Step 4. Pull down the center plate and take out the **sufferscreen** and filter. Replace it with a new one. Don't go Hadley with this—good **sufferfilters**, while simple, are crucial to the forward motion of your car. If your filter doesn't have newfound sounds and sunrise expressions, don't even install it.

Step 5. Replace the bolts and make sure that you've got a good seal. Is there any space for suffering? If so, loosen the bolts, reset the gasket and tighten the bolts again.

Step 6. Open the sufferoil and pour it in. Don't touch it or contaminate it in any way. And again, make sure that it is good oil. Good sufferoil will be fine, almost cocky, when you pour it. You want it to be saying things like, "No *sweat*," or, "Fuck it—this is no *problem*." If it's hedging (talking about a loved one, asking questions like, "Are you sure this is a good idea?") don't use it.

Step 7. Start the car and run it. Your VW should immediately look and act more confident. Good, clean sufferoil is absolutely essential to the happiness of your Volkswagen.

COAL MINER'S DAUGHTER

But what could I do? I just couldn't traipse all over western Massachusetts, searching every streetsong, sidewalk, and parking space for the shadow of a pasture or the flash of a farm—I didn't have the car for it! By then the VW could barely make it to Hatfield without breaking down—how could I have told that story?

So I made a decision.

First, I traded some time for a saw—a metal, bendy musical one. Then, one afternoon a few days after our visit to the hospital, I dropped the VW off at the Chest of Drawers' apartment. The VW begged to know where I was going, but I wouldn't tell him. I had to take this trip alone.

I walked down 47, towards South Hadley, and followed an offtrail up Summit Mountain. I climbed to the top and sat myself down on a rock. There I could see the sun armpitting back into the Pioneer Valley.

I knew what I had to do. I clenched my teeth, plunged my hand into my chest and took out my heart. It was small in my hand, and it beat furiously in the cold mountain air. I put it down on the rock and I left it there. Then I looked for a place to hide. I walked down a slight hill and over to a military monument which stood about a hundred feet away. I crouched behind the monument and waited.

Time passed. The moon crept up into the sky. I could see it staring at me and my heart, now softly beating on the rock.

In the middle of the night a picnic table tottled over to the heart. He looked around, sniffed the ground, and macked over to me. "Yo," he said to me.

"Hi," I said, trying to sound innocent.

The table nodded towards the rock. "Someone dropped their heart back there," he said.

"I'm sorry?"

"Is that your heart over there?"

"Oh," I said. I pretended to check my pockets for it, and then my chest. "Sheesh. It must have fallen out of my chest by mistake or something."

"You should grab it," he said. "There are trees that *eat* hearts up here."

"I'll go get it right now," I said.

But I didn't, of course. I stayed crouched behind the monument, my saw in my hand, waiting.

Sure enough, a tree crawled towards the heart around five or six that morning. The tree was thin and small and his face was grey.

I leaned forward. Was that *him*? He was so much smaller than I'd expected. I looked around for an Atkin's but I didn't see one.

The tree, meanwhile, silked tentatively towards the rock. He stopped about ten feet from it, sniffed the air and looked around. Then he stepped forward.

As he reached for the heart I ran towards him, screaming and swinging my singing saw. The tree put his limbs up. I pounced, throwing all of my weight at him. He fell and I dug my shoulders into his chest and put my saw to his wooden throat.

It was then that I felt the tree's birchy skin and read his ancient face.

"Please, please!" he begged. He had a British accent.

This *couldn't* be the same tree.

"Were you going to steal that heart?" I hissed. "Hah?"

"It was just lying there on the rock!" he stammered. "I'm just so hungry is all."

I dug the saw into his throat. "You're murderers—all of you," I said.

"What? All of who?"

"One of your brothers stole my *father,* took *his* heart."

"Who? I don't know what you're—"

"He's driving a *farm*. An Atkin's. Do you know him?" I pressed the saw into his white skin.

The old tree howled. "Is he a birch?"

"What?"

"A birch!"

"How the fuck would I know that?"

"Where does he live?"

"He drives a farm. An *Atkin's* Farm."

"I—no. No I don't."

I cut him. "You're full of *sap,*" I said.

"Really—I don't," the tree said. "I promise—I would tell you."

I picked up my tiny heart with my free hand and held it for the tree to see.

"I honestly didn't know that was your heart," the tree stammered. "I would never have taken it if I had known."

I didn't care—I dug the saw deeper into his skin. The tree screamed as I cut him in two, and his sap ran over the stone and onto the dirt path.

The song of that tree's death rang out from my saw on Summit Mountain and rained down over the Valley. I hoped that somewhere, my Heart Attack Tree was hearing it, that he was realizing his fate, and that he was frightened.

I cut that tree into tiny logs and I left him there in a pile. Then I put my heart back in my chest and walked down the mountain.

BOW LAKE, NEW HAMPSHIRE

And now all of these ideas are coming to me—all of these stories.

One winter, I rented a small cabin on Bow Lake, New

Hampshire—miles and miles away from Northampton—and the VW and I spent a week out there, walking along the deserted dirt roads that ran around the lake, reading books, renting movies and doing the things we were always too busy to do at home.

We'd gone there, though, because my son was growing more ill. Areas of his skin—his armpits, his neck—had started to turn brown. He had a terrible cough, and sometimes his scanner misfed stories. Often, he had trouble sleeping or lost track of time. Then, the VW and I were having breakfast at a diner called the Northwood and I struck up a conversation with an old wood stove. I told him a little about our situation—where we'd come from, that we were here on vacation, what we were vacationing *from* (Those days I spent most of my time either chasing stories for the *Wheel* or going to auditions with the VW, who'd decided in the months prior that he wanted to be an actor.). When the stove saw the VW shivering on his stool he said, "Looks like that kid could use a mechanic."

I said, "You know of one?"

The stove nodded. "Cod's name is Jerome. Lives at the bottom of the lake," he said, "but he's good." The stove gave me the mechanic's number, and I called him that very same day. I told him my son was a Volkswagen, explained his symptoms.

"Where you guys coming from?" said the voice on the phone.

"Western Mass—a town called Northampton."

"No, oh. Oh, I know Northampton," said the fish. "Did my cousin give you my number?"

"A wood stove that I met at the diner gave it to me."

"Your son's a Beetle?"

"A seventy-one," I said.

"Right. Buzzy told me about him. The actor, right?"

"I'm sorry?" I said.

"I've been to Northampton many times—mostly for auditions."

I was having trouble following him. "Can you fix him?"

"Oh. Oh, right, sure," said the Cod. "No problem. Bring him by—," he paused, "—how about Thursday?"

So I did; three days into our stay at Bow Lake, I helped the VW put on his wetsuit and we drove to the bottom of Bow Lake to see the fish mechanic. Deep we went, unconscious, hidden mind. It wasn't a big lake, and there were only a few businesses at the bottom, so the garage was easy to find. We pulled up to the bay door, waited for it to raise and drove in. Then the fish mechanic came into the garage and pulled the door closed behind us. He was dressed in a grey jumpsuit and a cigarette dangled from the corner of his mouth. His flippers were dirty with oil and his eyes carried stories of steel. He immediately approached the VW and extended his hand. "Mr. Volkswagen," he said.

The VW shook his hand but didn't say anything.

"I'm very, very excited to meet you," the Cod said. He stared at the VW and then at me. None of us said anything for a moment. Then the Cod pointed to the lift. "Let's get started, yes?"

My son rolled onto the lift and the Cod raised it. As the platform rose, the fish pretended to investigate my son's skin and engine. "Well," he said, broccoliing it. "A lot of skin color change."

"I'm pretty sure the problem's with one of the transmissions."

"I'm not sure about that—have you noticed all the rus–"

"Or the engineheart, which I *still* can't find," I said. "Can you give me any suggestions there?"

"For locating the engineheart?"

I nodded.

"It's very hard to explain— they're in different places in each car," he said.

"Well he's not burning right, or something. I tried to figure it out," I said, shaking my head, "but I just can't."

But that garage turned out to be a scam. After a few minutes, I realized that this mechanic was nothing more than a lonely old trout from another book, looking for a few more pages. Like most of the mechanics that I'd brought the VW to, this fucking fish didn't know the first thing about my son's storyengine—he looked at it as if he'd never even *seen* a story before. All he did was run a few tests—then he just stood there with his fins crossed, staring at the car.

I stepped up next to him. "You said it'd be no problem over the phone," I said.

He snapped his fingerfin. "Have you changed his memory oil?"

"His *suffer*oil?"

"Right, right. Have you changed that?"

"Of course I have—I change it every chapter."

The fish leaned towards me. "Hey—he still going to casting calls?"

I stepped back. "He's sick," I said. "He's really sick. You told me you could fix him. We made the trip down here."

The fish's eyes tried to send wires to mine. "Listen: This is a role, friend—it's just something I'm doing until something better comes along. Right?" He nodded at the VW. "He have an agent?"

"What?"

"No, nothing. I'm just, well—I'm just asking. I'm an actor, too, and I'm looking for—"

"Take my son down," I told him.

The fish's face grew cold. "I haven't figured out what's the matter yet," he said.

"Take him down, I said."

The fish mechanic walked guiltily over to the lever and lowered the lift, and the VW rolled off. His face was bright. "Am I fixed?" he said.

I didn't answer him; I just put his flippers back on and prepared him for the trip back up to the surface. As I did, the Cod sidled up to me. "Here's my card, at least," he said. "If you know anyone who needs an extra or something."

I ignored him; I finished putting the VW's wetsuit on and then I stepped into the driver's seat and closed the door. As I did, the Cod reached for the VW's hand and shook it. "It was a pleasure to meet you, Mr. VW," he said.

The VW smiled gently.

"I read a review of one of your performances in the *Wheel*. I was very impressed."

"Let's go," I said. I pulled the VW out of the bay and the fish closed the garage door behind us.

As we coasted along the lake bottom, the VW pressed me for details. "Didn't he say *anything*?"

"No."

"Did you tell him about my *skin*?"

"Yes."

"And he had no reaction?"

I didn't answer him.

"It's something serious, isn't it?" the VW said.

"He's not a real mechanic, kiddo," I said. "He's never even seen a storyengine before."

The VW pounded his blue fist on the watery pavement. "Why is it that no one has ever seen my engine before?" he said, his voice quivering. He glared at me. "What's *wrong* with me?"

Soon I would accept the fact that it was futile—that neither I nor any of the mechanics that I visited knew exactly what was wrong with the Volkswagen. My son was a mystery.

"Nothing, buddy—there's nothing wrong with you," I promised him. I turned the pagewheel and steered him up, up, up towards the bright surface.

TROUBLE, TROUBLE, TROUBLE

Not long after I spoke with him, the Cooley-Dickinson Hospital was found dead in his hospital bed, his face stumped beyond recognition. Two Dogs were guarding the door at the time, but the Tree got in anyway—by scaling the building, apparently. The Dogs heard the smashing of glass, but by the time they got inside the Tree was gone, Cooley-Dickinson defaced.

I went to the funeral, stood in the last pew at the Smith College Chapel, watched the hospital's father—the distinguished BayState Hospital, from Springfield—shake with grief in the front row, his old windows weeping into his white beard. I stared at the giant, hospital-shaped casket, my mind dividing itself into parts. Which sections should I keep? And which sections must go?

I'll keep *this* and *this*. To hell with the rest of it.

Cooley-Dickinson's sister, a paint store in New Haven, gave the eulogy. "When I think back to Cody," she said, grimacing through tears, "I just try to forget the last years, these last croons. I think Cody would want that. The *Wheel* might regard him as the victim of a Tree, but I remember the Cody who finished hospital school a year early; the Cody who, before this whole thing started, loved to draw comics, and was excited about the upcoming release of his first comic book series, *STAT*."

Then the paint store coda'd into a southern maine—a plastic review about the hospital's comic book, which was set, fittingly, in a hospital. She described the first issue, a funny thin side about a dying basketball which had the audience craughing.

I just kept thinking, this hospital was *an artist*. A brother, a son. And look what I/the tree had done to him.

I accompanied the funeral party to the cemetery and watched them lay the hospital into the ground. After the service, I approached the old hospital and offered him my hand. I looked into his old rooms and started to tell him who I was, who my father was, but he put up his hand and said, "I knew who you were, Mr. _____, the minute you walked into the church."

"I just wanted to say how sorry—"

"No," he said, his voice trembling. "Don't give *me* your sorries. You tell them to my *son*."

I was silent.

"You go there," he said, pointing to the giant hole in the earth, "and you tell Cody that you're sorry."

I stammered a response.

"Mr. ____," the old hospital said, leaning over me. "Why *these* stories? Why this one, in particular?"

By then other mourners had stopped to hear our discussion. "I—I don't follow."

"You don't *follow*? How about, for once, a *happy* tune? How about, a young promising hospital gets renovated, or gets married, or—"

"You sound like my son," I said. "This is what he tells me, too."

"He's right," the old hospital said. "You should listen to him."

"Sir," I said, my voice just a note above a whisper. "These stories chose me. *They* chose *me*."

"Then ignore them!"

"Ignore them?"

"People's lives are at stake here!" he coaled.

"I've *tried*. If it were only that simple."

"Then run. Run away. Go somewhere where these stories can't find you."

"I've tried that, too," I said. "But they're faster. They find me every time.

"I've tried *everything*," I told him.

I WOULD DIE FOR YOU

I'm thinking back, going back in my mind, to that Sunday in the fall of 2004, when the Memory of My Father and I went to the flee bee—the Old Hadlee Flea Market, held every week on a small farm on Route 47—and he bought a small war in a beautiful little wooden trinket box.

Was that in '04—so long ago already?

Yes, I think it was, because it was the same day that I bought the corpse of an old accordion who'd gotten in a bar fight and been stabbed and killed. I bought it from a moustached truck who was selling it for two and a half hours. "No guarantees," he said as I handed over the time. He put the coffin in my arms; the instrument's bellows were stiff, its keys cold and grey.

My hope, though, was that I might be able to fix the accordion and

170

convince the VW to take lessons on it. I'd always loved the accordion, and so had my father. I brought the musicorpse home and began working on it—I opened its skin at the seam, fed it fluids and nutrients intravenously, repaired its organs with epoxy and c-clamps, replaced two of its buttons, sewed its wounds and reattached its skin—and a few days later it opened its eyes and looked into my face.

"Oh god thank you," he said, weeping.

But then the VW refused to play. That night—the night the accordion was resurrected—I put on some Cajun music for the VW to listen to, and he heard two notes and said that it was the least cool thing he'd ever heard.

"You don't like this stuff?" I said.

"People actually *listen* to this?" the VW said.

"It's nice—it's folky, happy," I said.

"It's a rose bush making fart sounds with its elbow," the VW said.

So I had to kill the accordion all over again. The next morning, I set up a noose and a small stool in the front yard. I had the instrument stand in place on the stool while I slipped the rope around his neck.

He flailed his tiny, keyed hands. "Please, no!" he begged.

"My son doesn't want you," I told him. "I really thought he would."

"I need to live!" the accordion said.

"But for what purpose?" I reasoned with him. "Who will play you?"

I could see his mind working. He stammered for an answer, but my job was clear and I did what needed to be done: I stepped back and kicked out the stool. The noose tightened. The accordion's eyes went wide. He coughed—"Gack! god—Gack!"—and then his hands fell and his head slumped forward.

I kept him hanging there for a week, as a warning to other instruments. A few days later I was sitting by the window and I saw a French horn walking past on the sidewalk stop cold when he noticed the re-killed and hung accordion. His face was filled with fear.

At the end of the week I took the accordion down, laid him in his coffin and buried him. I wonder whether I'll see him again.

But I was talking about the trinket box with the war inside, the one the Memory of My Father bought at the flee bee that day. As I said, he didn't mean to buy the war; he was just interested in the box, which was made of spruce and had some very interesting designs carved in the lid. As near as I could tell, the woodcuts told a story—a story about a chariot in the Old West. There was one scene with the chariot in a duel, his wide-brimmed hat cocked back and his hand hovering over his holster.

I was there when the Memory of My Father bought it, from a young girl who was watching the table while her mother went for coffee. He paid only twenty minutes for it, because the box was locked and the girl said the key had been lost. The Memory of My Father bought it and tucked it under his arm and the two of us walked proudly back to the car—he with his storybox, me with my coffined accordion.

It wasn't until about a half an hour later, as we were driving home, that I picked up the box to study the scenes and heard noises coming from inside it. I put the box to my ear and I could hear booms and crashes.

I held the box out to the Memory of My Father, who was steering with one hand and holding a jelly donut with the other. "Listen to this," I said. I held it to his ear.

"I just hear shifting," he said.

"There's something happening inside this box," I declared. I tried again to open it, but couldn't. "I'm going to open this thing up and see what's inside it."

"You do that and you're going to fuck up the lock, and it won't be worth anything," the Memory of My Father said. "Just leave it be, _____."

"I won't fuck up a thing," I said. "I'll be careful."

The Memory of My Father shook his head and bit into his donut.

Later that day, the VW and I went down to my Dad's workbench in the basement of the Crescent Street house and we tried to loosen the lock. I let the VW try first—he tried to pick the lock with a paper-clip, and then he took a tiny flathead screwdriver and tried to pry the catch.

But I grew impatient, and after ten minutes or so I went and grabbed a crowbar. "Give me that thing," I told him.

"Don't use that—you're going to snap the latch right off," the VW said.

"I won't—I'll be careful."

"Dad—"

"Give it," I said, and I took the box from him. I stuck the prybar against the latch and turned it, which created a little gap between the two halves. I heard moans inside.

"What's that sound?" the VW said.

The latch wouldn't give. I pushed hard on the crowbar once, twice.

"Careful—"

"I'm being careful," I said, and pushed again, but this time the wood cracked.

We both stared at what I'd done.

"Did I tell you?" the VW said.

I'd pried the lock right out of the wood, ruined the lid. I said a custom-made swear.

"Didn't I tell you not to use the crowbar?" the VW said.

"Just don't tell the Memory of My Father," I said.

"Like he won't know."

"He won't know, not if you don't tell him," I said. "I'm sick of you two conspiring against me."

"What?" the VW said.

"Everyone in this *engine* is conspiring against me," I said.

"Dad," the VW said. His face was plaid. "Do you really think that?"

I heard a soft *boom* inside the box, and then small voices.

"Are you going to open that thing, or what?" the VW said.

"I'm getting to it," I told him. "Don't push me—I'll open it when I'm goddamn good and ready."

"Alright, alright," the VW said.

I slowly opened the lid and we both peered inside. Immediately I knew what we were looking at.

"It's a *war*," I whispered.

It was night inside the box—the stars and the moon hung below me. Tiny men the size of eyelashes were running across a field. Then, the crack and flash of a bomb. All of the running men stopped and froze, then dropped back behind a hill. Gunshots came, and a new team of men surrounded them.

All of the soldiers were of one mind. You could see it in their faces as they aimed and fired, ran and hid, destroyed the hearts of others, lost their legs and eyes and either a) died or b) did not die.

The VW pulled back from the box and his face shawled. "What are they doing?" he said.

I was upset, of course. What was this war *about*? And what was I supposed to do with it?

"They're fighting," I said.

"What for?" the VW said.

"It's a disagreement of some kind."

"Over what?"

"I don't know the specifics," I told him. "It could be anything."

The VW didn't say anything. He stared into the box, at the dead on the field, and then he looked down at his shoes. "Can I go to my room?"

I felt guilty all of a sudden. "Sure you can, buddy," I said.

I placed the lid back on the box and I called the Memory of My Father, and he came over an hour later. He sat down on a stool in front of the box. "Open it," I told him.

"What'd you do here?" he said, pointing to the lid.

"I don't know how that happened," I said.

"You tried to pry it open, didn't you?" the Memory of My Father said.

"I didn't touch it—the VW must have done that," I told him.

• • •

We kept the war going through the fall. The Memory of My Father left the box in the basement, and every few days I would check on it and see what was happening. Many lives were lost. The sun rose and fell. I looked to see if there might be any end in sight, but I didn't have the whole thing—this box was apparently only one piece of a much larger conflict—so I never knew who was who and whether one side was making more progress than the other.

One Sunday that winter, the Memory of My Father met an antiques collector at an estate sale. He told this man about the box and the designs on the front, and the collector said he'd like to see it. The Memory of My Father called me that afternoon and told me to clear out the war so that he could show the box to the collector.

"How am I supposed to do that?" I asked.

"You're a big boy, you can figure it out," the Memory of My Father said. "Just scoop it out."

Something inside me was sad. "Did you tell him about the lock?"

"Bah," the Memory of My Father said. "He won't even notice it."

I thought long and hard about how to get rid of the war—I didn't want to just pour it out. Instead, I put the box in the freezer, thinking that all of the soldiers would freeze and die, and then I could dump the whole thing into the trash—hills and bunkers and bodies and all.

But somehow the soldiers survived the cold. I opened the box after two days in the freezer and I saw a division dressed in fur, marching stiffly along a perimeter. By this point I was using a magnifying glass (which I borrowed from my son's science kit) to see closer, and I could see every face as individual and unique. I saw two men huddled together for warmth and another a few feet away, writing a letter. I snatched it from his hand and read it.

Things get worse all the time. This cold front is upon us and every day we lose more men. My Sergeant says that we will never give up, never die, but if I can't get warm soon I don't think I'll make it.

I think back to home. Remember the shower day? That Tuesday before the concert? I think of you and how warm that was.

God, my hands. I can't hold the pen. Have to go. I'll write again tonight.
Love

I brought the box with me when I went home that night for dinner and I held it out to the Memory of My Father. "The war's still in there," I told him.

"What?" he said. "I told you to clear it out."

"I tried to freeze them but it didn't work."

"Just get them out of there, what the fuck!" the Memory of My Father said. Then he took the box under his arm and went outside. The late afternoon sun was a piece of candy. The Memory of My Father turned on the hose and opened the box. All of the fighting stopped and the soldiers looked up into their sky, past their sun and into the Memory of My Father's face. He sprayed the inside hard, until all the dead bodies and the hills and streams and stars and moon were pushed out onto the pavement, and within minutes the box was completely empty. With his holy hose, The Memory of My Father forced them down the driveway and towards the gutter at the curb.

The antiques collector didn't buy the box—he was upset when he saw that it had a broken lock—and so the Memory of My Father brought it home and stored it in his garage.

A few years later I found the box again, dusty and stashed in a corner. I opened it up and peered inside. I saw six or seven men huddled around a fire. I think there was a crude map of some sort at their feet. It looked to me as if they were making plans.

ENGINE STOPS OR WON'T START

There are several reasons why your Volkswagen might stall, stop or not start. The most common culprits are the **fuel injection system** (**pump, condenser**) or a glitch in the **timing**. But don't overlook the possibility that it might also be a malfunctioning **control unit**—a much more serious problem.

MECHANICS

First, there may be a problem with the **ignition**, "How to Use This Book." Have you reviewed it to make sure that it reads at the right speed?

Second, it's possible that the scene clutch is failing to engage with one of the transmissions. To check the linkage, press your ear to the page and knock on it. Do you hear a hollow echo or the sound of metal against metal? If it's the latter, the linkage—or the page—is probably twisted. You can either reshape the page by hand or get underneath the car, drop the transmissions, and use a pair of april-plyers to straighten out the twisted parts.

If both the linkage and the ignition appear to be OK, though, your next step should be to check the timing. The quickest way to do so is to open the engine compartment and take a look at the sun and moon(s). Watch them through at least one cycle (no matter how long it takes). Then decide: Are they timed correctly? Volkswagens have more problems with engine timing than any other car I know of—they constantly fall behind or speed forward, or slip from one version to another (both inside the engine compartment and on the road—in the story—itself!). My 1971 Beetle was notorious for this—I can't tell you how many times we drifted unknowingly from one speed to the next. One minute the sun was hanging still in the sky, the next the moon was swimming laps around the earth. And I'll never forget the time we found ourselves on a road on which the time wasn't moving *at all!*

My advice is to try and avoid these situations if at all possible. There are ways to adjust the time if you find yourself lost in a shift, but most drivers in that situation simply keep their eyes on their surroundings—the traffic, the scenery, the road—and do their best to adjust.

FUEL EFFICIENCY

The most likely scenario is that there's something wrong with your **fuel system**, though, so let's review it.

First, check your stories. Are they burning quickly and completely? Sometimes, in order to render a story more likely to be burned, you need to strip an actual occurrence—a "true" story—down to its frame. Take "Rear Differential" for example, which I fed the VW out of desperation on one of our most trying trips, the wild chase west. That part was built from a change that actually did happen to me. I really did have a friend—not a bull but a barricade—who drove out to Hampshire College while we were both students in Boston, and he *did* have a jug of wine that he kept hoisting up and drinking out of as we drove. It was a cold night and I remember dropping him off at a lonely hut-like dorm at Hampshire, watching him knock on the front door, the potato on his face as he looked back at me, unsure if his friend was inside or not. Then the warm door opened and he slipped inside, and I drove off towards Smith, where my girlfriend at the time was waiting for me.

I saw this friend years later, in fact, his blond hair tamed and his face imprisoned by glass and metal. The Mechanical Bull was working in the city as a banker, his muscles pressed into a skintight grey suit.

My point is, the real story is soft and it licks your face but the one I fed the VW carries water and minerals—a bull, some hope, a home. But the vertebrae—the trip, the wine, the eyes, the campus—are in place, distilled and even truer than I remember them to be.

And why this particular story, this tune? I can't say for sure why the VW chose it to burn, but I do know what drove me to tell it to him. There was real rubble to it; I was excited to be with this Bull, who I admired, and also frightened that his drinking might get us in trouble. The car felt smart and Hampshire felt like home, and it was one of those nights that I wished would pass but now would trade almost anything to return to.

None of these complicated procedures reach the surface, but they're always happening nonetheless; words are burning, experiences changing, information is being transformed to actual motion. Even now, I still find that pretty amazing.

CONTROL UNIT

If the Volkswagen has fuel, its timing is set properly and each of the components of the fuel system—the minutepump, the sensors, the feeder and the morning cables leading to and from the **compressor** and **expansion tank**—seem to be working, you may have a problem with the

control unit, which is to say that the VW might be stalling or not starting because he or she *doesn't want* to move forward. They may be confused, mentally ill, overly cautious or simply upset about something.

I ran into this situation more than once with my car. In his third year, the 1971 VW grew tired of our routines—going to and from home, work and my parents' house in Longmeadow. Then he heard Cooley-Dickinson's song and he begged me to follow it. "How can you continue to spool around Northampton when the tune clearly goes west?" he said to me one evening as were driving to Hadley, where I was meeting a woman for dinner.

"Who says the farm went west?" I said. "You don't know that for sure."

"It's what the hospital said," the VW said. "It's what we *saw* at the Castaway."

"We've been over this," I said. "I really don't think that was the same farm."

"It *was* the same farm," said the Volkswagen. "I told you it was but you wouldn't listen to me."

I shrugged. "If it was then the Dogs will find him—they said they'd resume their search, didn't they?"

"Still," the VW said. "Why can't we try too?"

"Because I said so," I said.

"But *why?*"

"Because we'd have to drive fast—"

"So?"

"—and the only way we could get west fast would be to take ninety-one north to two," I said.

"Let's do that, then!"

"I told you," I said. "Ninety-one is off limits. There's too much sound!"

"Too much sound? I can handle it," he said.

"No you can't," I said.

"You never give me any credit," the VW said.

"It's not a matter of credit," I said. "What if we broke down?"

"We won't break down."

"We *always* break down," I said.

"We won't this time."

"You're damn right we won't, because we're not going," I said.

"How come I'm healthy enough to drive *you* places, but never to go anywhere I want to go?"

"Enough, OK? I said no."

The VW mumbled something.

"What?" I said.

"Nothing," he said.

"No, what?"

"*Nothing*," he said again.

"It *better* have been nothing," I said.

The VW was quiet for a minute, and so was I. I twisted the rearview mirror so that I could see my face. Then I said, "I feel nauseous—do I look pale?"

"Pale?"

"Am I underdressed?"

"You're fine, jeez," the VW said, and he took a right into the parking lot of the restaurant. This was Sienna—that fancy pasta cord a few miles from Amherst Center. The woman I was meeting—a Lady Made Entirely of Stained Glass (See "Valve Adjustment")—was already there, waiting by her stained glass car.

I stepped out of the VW. "Hi," she said.

"Hi," I said, and I gave her a quick hug. She waved to the VW.

"Yo," he said, his eyes oceaning.

Over the next few weeks, though, the VW became increasingly rambunctious, complaining of boredom and begging for trips. When I refused to give in he tried a new tactic: convincing me he was too sick to be my car. He'd complain of dizziness, halfburn or weak skin, fake an illness or a breakdown, pull over without warning, pretend to vomit or pass out from exhaustion. At first I was fooled—or *fueled* (hah!)—and I'd try to fix him: I'd get out of the car, grab my diagnostic tools and check his sensors, his morning cables, his oil. But soon I realized what he was up to and I stopped responding. When we broke down I'd simply wait for him to smarten up and get back on the road. Sometimes these charades went on for hours; once I even waited overnight. Sure enough, his engine turned over at around six the next morning and he drove us home without saying a word to me.

But the VW was so *stubborn*, so determined to make me change, and when he realized that the fake breakdowns wouldn't do it he raised the stakes by breaking down at only the most critical of times; once, on our way to cover a story for the *Wheel*, another on a drive in the country with the Lady Made Entirely of Stained Glass, another when I was fleeing an enemy.

This was the worst one, because my life was literally in danger. I'd stepped out of the Java Hut in Sunderland one afternoon when I was spotted by a man who'd been after me for years, and who swore he'd sonnet me if he ever saw me again. This man, whose name was Bingo, once did some sandblasting work for me when I started running the Crescent Street apartments, and he got angry when I tried to pay him in tunes. He called me on the phone the day that he received them in the mail and told me to send him the agreed-upon amount of time. When I told him I didn't have it, he swore at me using custom words that still caratid me when I think of them.

Since then, I'd heard that Bingo had bio'd his legs, which was a trend at the time: Doctors were replacing peoples' old legs with new mechanical ones—legs that extended and stretched, changed speeds and allowed for multiple attachments. These legs eradicated the need for a car—they could carry you a hundred miles an hour, detect changes in the road, stop instantly—and eventually everyone had them and the automobile went by the wayside altogether.

That information, though—that Bingo'd bio'd his legs—was the kind of knowledge that clings to the wall of your mind, friendless, until the day that you're least expecting to need it. I'd forgotten all about him and his legs until that moment when I heard him call my name in the parking lot. Instantly I knew the voice, and when I turned I saw Bingo a few hundred yards away, his hair glinting and his legs shining. He pointed at me and I immediately dropped my coffee and sprinted to the

Volkswagen, fumbling for my keys. Then I heard the *whirr* of the BioLegs as Bingo fired them up.

I jumped into the driver's seat and slammed the door behind me. "VW, go!" I yelled.

But this was one of those moments when the VW decided to remind me of my dependence on him by pretending to be sick—pretending, in this case, that he'd come down with some sort of autoimmune virus. When I turned the key he faked a shiver and a cough. His eyes were half-closed.

"Go, go, go!" I yelled.

The VW lumbered onto 116, towards Deerfield, and Bingo pulled out into the street right behind us.

"We need to move faster, kiddo," I said.

"I can't *go* any faster!" he tourniqueted.

I took the wheel in one hand and the clutch in the other. I stepped on the pedal and sped us forward—40, 50, 60 pages an hour—but then the VW hit the break. In my rearview mirror I could see Bingo's legs spinning like seeds.

"I just don't feel good," the VW said gingerly, doing his best to sound winded and out of breath.

"Not now, VW!" I yelled. "Don't you recognize that guy? Do you realize what he's going to do if he catches me?"

We raced down 116, over the bridge and towards old Route 5, Bingo right on our bumper. As we passed 47, though, he fell about a car-length behind. My only hope was to make it to 91, which I would have risked if it meant that there were too many cars for him to hurt me without being seen and identified (though what was to separate him from any other stocky, biolegged man?). We weren't very far from the entrance—maybe a mile, tops.

Right at the intersection of 116 and 5, though, the VW sputtered. I yelled for him to keep going but he pulled over. His eyes were slits. "I *can't*," he kept saying. I still remember the way he said it, his voice a box of salt. "I just *can't*."

"VW! Not now!"

"It must have been something I ate—my stomach hurts so much," he said.

I jumped out of the car and the VW turned over on his side.

"This is all in your *mind*," I told him.

"No," the VW murmured, and he closed his eyes.

"Just shift from one version to another!" I said.

But the VW was unconscious—he wasn't faking it this time.

I heard Bingo pull to a stop and I turned to face him. He was smiling and hovering a few inches off the ground. He crossed his arms. "_____! How *nice*! Long time no see," he said, grinning.

I stammered to make conversation. "You had—your legs—"

"Yes! An upgrade!" he said.

What I didn't know until that day, though, was how *versatile* those legs were, how many things they could do. Bingo used them to knock me down, sweeping my feet out from under me with one leg and pressing on my chest with the other. He held me down with one foot and extended the other high. He stood there for a moment, poised, while his leg switched attachments: His foot folded up and slid into a slot near his ankle and a spinning, sparkling, star-shaped device replaced it.

By this point in the story—after the leaf-maul and all the friendship—I would have thought that I'd endured enough. But Bingo apparently felt differently. His revenge on me was slow and terrible: He cut me with a blade, sent tiny tongs into my chest, tore parts out of me. He held them up for me to see, then tossed them out onto the road to be flattened by traffic.

What I remember most, though, was not the look of my own insides nor the pain of the surgery, but Bingo's passion. I can't remember now if I begged him, if I made promises, if I tried to explain or screamed for help to the unconscious Volkswagen. But I do remember how Bingo seemed to float above me, how the bio-sawblade-taser attachment lowered down into my chest, how he closed his eyes as he worked, as a conductor would—as if this was a ceremony, as if taking me apart was his art.

Those weeks after the death of the hospital were very busy for me. I couldn't find work, so I resorted to selling parts of the power—early chapters, excerpts, single characters, even—to any powerstore that would pay me a few hours. Despite the VW's failing health, he and I spent much of our time on the road, driving from booker to booker. Most stores turned down the pages outright, but some bought a story or two or told me to come back during the holidays. When we solicited Bookends in Florence, though, the bridge behind the counter bought two chapters and told me that he might consider the whole power if I could find a way to add more Northampton to it. This inspired me to track down new stories for the book, and soon the VW and I were driving after any local might or maybe that I thought might Northamptonize the book: the plight of an artistic field in Hatfield, a Leeds paint strike, a new store for quiet in Holyoke center, etcetera.

These stories weren't easy to find—they never are!—and the trips were difficult for the VW. Some of them were far—we read through Sunderland, Huntington, Chicopee Falls—and the VW would have to take frequent breaks to nap or cough up oil. Some tunes were productive, but others were wild storychases down strange antiroads which led us, when we reached the supposed destination, to the Memory or Promise of a story but *no actual story*. There were many days, then, when we came back to Northampton with nothing.

As the weeks passed, the VW stopped bothering me about the Castaway or lobbying to follow the Tree west. In fact, he grew steely quiet and hardly spoke to me at all. We often drove in silence, and when we got home from a storytrip the VW usually went right to his room while I made a cup of chai and sat down in the living room to read, write or revise. I knew that my son was still carrying a grudge, but I expected that to change—soon, I predicted, he would forget about missing fathers and farms and focus his energies elsewhere.

Which is exactly what happened when, early that winter, the VW developed an interest in engineering. Somewhere along the way, he'd picked up a book on the subject at one of the used bookstores. He read that book cover to power, and was soon buying other books on the subject, which he carried in his front compartment and read while he was waiting for me. He didn't talk to me about what he was reading, but I saw from the books' covers that one of them was about small engine repair and another about automotonal technology.

Soon, he'd turned his room/garage into a workshop and started building projects; he spent all his free time using materials I didn't recognize to build machines I didn't understand. He wouldn't tell me what these projects were—he was still not really speaking to me—and I didn't want to pry, but one Saturday afternoon I was in the kitchen making soup when the VW opened his bedroom door and said, "Hey Dad?"

"Yo," I said.

"Remember when we used that outboard motor to get through the Main Street canal?"

"'Shimmies and Shakes?'"

The VW nodded.

"You just fastened the engine to the sheet metal, right?"

"Right," I said.

"Cool," he said, and he started to close the door.

"Wait a second," I said. "Why?"

"Just curious," he said, and slammed the door.

One day soon after that, I heard muted construction noises—singsong saws, choruses of hammers—coming from the VW's room. I knocked on the door, and when the VW appeared his face was sooty. "What?" he said.

"What's going on in there?" I said. "I hear the sound of carpentry. What are you doing?"

"Nothing," he said.

I put my hands on my hips.

"I'm just listening to music is all," said the VW.

There was a smell coming from his room—the smell of welding. "What kind of *music*?"

"Just—a band, Dad, alright?"

"What band?"

"The—" The VW paused, and then his face brightened. "The Carpenters."

"Oh," I said. "Cool." That made sense. The Carpenters were a real band who made music in the 1970s—One Side of My Mother used to sing me their songs.

I should have read the roadsigns—should have remembered that The Carpenters, despite their name, did not really make construction-style music. Or I should have asked more questions when, a few days later, a problem came to the door with some sheets of tin. "Delivery for a Mister—" he read the paperwork— "Nineteen seventy-one—"

"That's for me," said the VW, coughing. He signed for the delivery, picked up the tin and carried it back to his bedroom/garage.

"Wait a second," I said. "What's all that tin for?"

The VW ignored me.

"VW," I said.

The VW turned towards me, and his face audited my face. "You know what?" he said. "It's a surprise. A present! It's for a present for you. OK?"

"A *present*?"

"For your birthday," the VW. "Alright?"

"Seriously?" I said. "Is that why you've been so secretive?"

The VW just stared at me.

This did strike me as strange—my birthday wasn't for six months—but I didn't question it at the time. "Wow—that's really thoughtful of you, kiddo," I said. "I won't even try to guess what it is then. That way I can be surprised!"

The VW gave me a thumbs-up sign, picked up the sheets of tin and carried them into his room.

He spent the entire next day in his room with the door closed. That night, I was sitting in the living room, reading a diagnostic about wind narratives—stories written and composed, entirely, of wind—when the VW opened the door. Billows of smoke spilled into the living room. "VW!" I said. "What are you doing in there?"

"I was—reading," he said.

"What's all that smoke from?"

"What smoke?" the VW said.

"I smell smoke," I said.

"You do? I don't," said the VW.

I shook my head and went back to my reading.

The VW stepped into the living room. "I'm going to sleep now," he said.

"OK. Goodnight," I said.

He didn't move. "Dad?" he said.

I looked up from my reading.

The VW's eyes were bleary. "Can I say something?"

"Sure," I said.

He seemed to weigh his words carefully. "Just, sorry for all the trouble I've caused you."

"What—the noise?" I said.

The VW idled.

"No problem," I said. "It sounds like you're really taking an interest in carpentry composition, which is great. Your grandfather would be really proud of you."

I turned back to my reading, but when I looked up again the VW was still standing there. "You OK?" I said.

His engine stalled. "This was always the way it was supposed to go. OK?"

"I don't know what you're talking about," I said. "The way *what* was supposed to go?"

"The next chapter," he said.

"Wait—what?" I said. "What about the next chapter?"

"The futuresongs," he said.

"VW," I said, "Can this wait? I'm in the middle of this excursion on literary windstorms. Can we talk about this another time?"

His eyes wednesdayed. "Sure we can," he said.

He went to his room, and I turned back to my reading about the wind. It was a captivating chapter. Was *this* was the problem with my power—that it lacked wind? Every word in my stories just *sat* there on the page, not moving at all.

For a few minutes after that I heard the sounds of construction from the VW's room—the revving of engines, the whining of a saw. Then the noise stopped, and the apartment was completely quiet.

GOLD RUSH

That morning, I woke up early and booked for a while. I'd collected a few Northamptons over the past weeks, as the bookstore bridge had suggested, but fitting them into the book was another matter—I often had to bend the stories, or break them and reshape them. I began that particular day by taking out the ogeltree to clean it, but then I snapped a piece of the plastic by mistake. I called around and found a place that had one—Amherst Typewriter—and then I knocked on the VW's door. It was only eight in the morning, so I assumed that he was still asleep. "Storytime, VW," I said.

The VW often slept late, and sometimes slept through the day if he was sick, but he usually mumbled something—a custom-made, a u-turn-term—when I woke him up. That morning, though, he didn't say anything.

"Kiddo," I said, "we need to get to Amherst—I need an ogeltree for the book. Can we leave in ten minutes?"

Again, no answer.

"Hey." I knocked again. "Ten minutes, OK?"

I put my ear to the door. "VW?" I didn't hear anything. "You're worrying me—are you OK?"

He wasn't answering.

"I'm going to open this door now, alright? VW? I'm opening the door."

I opened the door into a plume of engine parts, books, tools, maps.

But there was no VW. The VW was gone.

VIII. VOLKSWAGEN DOESN'T STOP

TRANSMISSION II (SLIPS AND JERKS)

Your Volkswagen will lead you through multiple versions—this version and others as well. Don't read this as a malfunction—this is how Volkswagen Beetles (and/or books about Volkswagen Beetles—Muir's, mine, or anyone else's) work! They move, they shift, they change.

Sometimes, though, one of the transmissions can *un*shift. You can lose ground. You shouldn't worry if your VW shifts or revises, but you should *absolutely* worry if the car stops shifting, or if the version stays constant. If that happens, something is wrong.

In the event of an unshift, open up the engine compartment and remove the **control unit**. Then, take out the **momentpump**. Underneath it you'll see a middle **transmission**, encased completely in glass. Some Beetle owners describe the transmission as taco-like—I've heard others say it looks like a bird in a glass coffin. Like I say, every car is different. Plus, the transmission is still a sort of mystery-vision for me—I know that it connects to the engineheart (where stories are bred), for example, but I can't say how. All I can tell you is that the transmission connects the story to the reader, and thus, that it's an integral part of the car.

If the transmission is unshifting, you may have a storylinkage problem, in which case something is keeping the story from moving forward. To investigate this, undo the sufferbolts around the edges of the glass casing and take a look inside. You'll see a series of interlocking narratives. Is there any schmutz between them, any wrinkle or disconnect that you can see?

Once, my car's transmission was malfunctioning because of a piece of storyfuzz, and as soon as I removed it the car ran like an awning. Usually, though, I'm not so lucky—it's more likely that you'll open the casing and find a narrative deteethed or twisted, in which case you'll need to order a replacement for it.

If you want to drive the car in the meantime, you're going to have to shift it yourself—to push the story forward manually.

Let's say, for example, that the story is:

Your son is a 1971 Volkswagen Beetle who has disobeyed you and left the house on his own. When you open the door to his room you find the **afterstory**: condensers, scraps of tin and steel, diagrams, translators, pages of verbs in various languages. These words are the first things you see, depaged and collected in a shoebox by the door. You pick up the box and look through the words: "mlape," "svesket," "marchon," "balinquoo," "quandary." There's not one term you recognize.

You step into the room and see strange engine components, some books about aerodynamics, a notebook full of sketches, charts and diagrams on the wall. You scan one of these charts, which appears to denote topographical musical notation. Another drawing, which is taped above the VW's worktable, appears to be a hand-drawn map. You study the jagged, intersecting lines. That crooked trail there appears to be a river, but which river?

Then you study the volksenscratch notes—here he's written the number two, and there the number five, and—

No.

Suddenly you see: This is a drawing of Route 91, from Northampton to Greenfield.

The Volkswagen has gone after the Heart Attack Tree.

That explains the maps, the engineering books, the projects. He wasn't working on a *birthday present,* but the very opposite—an unpresent, the gift that keeps on taking away.

Understand that your Volkswagen has no concept of the highway-song—what the tune is, how to hear it or steer it. He won't even know if he's in the verse or the chorus. And he's sick—he's very, very sick.

He won't make it to *Deerfield.*

And you, suddenly sans car, have no way to catch up with him. The narrative has unshifted.

Were that the case, you might shift the story manually, like this:

First Gear: The Volkswagen is your responsibility. This is *your* fault, and no one else's.

Second Gear: He will die in the sound if you don't find him.

Third Gear: What are you waiting for? There is not a second of time-of-money to waste.

Fourth Gear: Go! Go now.

GRINDS AND GROWLS (TRANSAXLE)

I grabbed the heavy power-in-pieces and ran out the door, down the hill to Prospect Street, over to King Street and towards the entrance to 91. In twenty minutes I was sprinting up the on-ramp, my mind a needle. Before I reached the top of the ramp, even, I could see the flush of vehicles—Veggies, bioleggers, riffs and phrases, traveling vests and fences, etcetera. The choruslanes were jammed; vehicles switched aggressively from one staff to the next and some even jumped over the driver in front of them. Up ahead, I saw a bioleger elbow a fence on its way past, and the fence spin onto the median.

It began to rain. I put my hands over my ears—the drops of sound were *deafening*.

I stuck out my thumb and began running along the breakdown lane. I was crying and waving for help, but no one would stop—VeggieCars and bio's shrilled past me, yelling insults out the window. "Get off the road, you crazy *vosk*," shouted a woman in a carcoat, and then a shower on bio's viced "Don't you know the storysong is only a *metaphor*?"

"For what?" I shouted back. She couldn't hear me, so the question ran along beside me. And it was just one of several: Did I really think I could catch the VW? That I would find my father this way? And which direction was I going, anyway—towards the past, or fast-forward towards a future?

Yes. Yes to every question. I was running towards my family, towards life. I believed—I still believe—that his heart was still beating. That *my* heart was still beating. That *your* heart is still beating.

• • •

I'd been sprinting along the highwaysong for about ten minutes when I suddenly saw a blue 1971 Volkswagen Beetle driving in the other direction. I stopped running and tried to flag it down. Thank god! "VW!" I shouted.

But the car was driving ethereally fast, and when it sped past me I saw that it was *brand new*—the notes bounced off of its shiny blue paint. This car wasn't my son. I stopped waving to it, and watched it disappear around the bend of the previous verse.

As I was standing there a jazzy, syncopated riff approached and pulled over. Inside was a trio of instruments—a piano in the front seat, a bass and drums in the back.

I was drenched by the musical rain, and I'd been weeping and mumbling so I'm sure my face was red and swollen. When the piano rolled down the film, he read my face and said, "Need a ride?"

I got into the riff. "Noisy night, huh?" the piano said, steering us back into traffic.

"Did you just come from Springfield?" I said.

"Hartford," said the bass fiddle.

"You didn't see a Volkswagen driving in the other direction, did you?"

"A what?" the drum set said. His voice was smoky and cracked.

"A Volkswagen," I said. "It's a kind of car. They're sort of round? This one's blue."

"Jesus," the drums said. "I've never even heard that *word* before."

"I think I might have seen one of those as a kid, in a museum somewhere," said the piano.

"Is that why you're out here?" said the bass. "Did you lose your car?"

"My son, yes," I said.

The bass asked, "Is he traveling south?"

"I don't think so—I think he's going north, towards Greenfield," I said. "But I'm not sure—he left home this morning and didn't tell me where he was going."

"He ran away?" the piano said, furrowing his wooden brow.

"It's a long story—a whole novel, actually, and this is the wrong version. He left to follow—to track—a farm."

"A *farm*?" the piano said.

I nodded. "And I *forbade* him from traveling on ninety-one. Who can navigate with all this *noise*?"

"Tell me about it," the drums said. "We weren't even supposed to have come this far—numb notes missed our exit a few miles back."

"Numb-notes," the bass said, smiling dumbly.

Then the drums leaned forward—I could feel him studying me. "What's that?" he said.

I looked back at him.

"That," he said, pointing.

"It's a power," I said.

"A power?"

"—book," I said. "I call it *How to Keep Your Volkswagen Alive*."

The piano shook his head and hunched over the riff's steering wheel. "It's pretty dischordant out here," he said.

"What's it do?" the drums said.

"Oh," I said. I looked down at the book. "I don't know. I always carry it with me. It holds stories."

"Does it project them, or—"

I shook my head.

"Does it do calculations or solve problems?" the drums asked.

"No—it just stores the experience."

"Converted?"

"No, raw," I said. I looked down at the book. "So it doesn't *do* much of anything, I guess."

The drums looked at the book with disdain.

"Sturdy," I said quietly.

"I'm sorry?" said the piano.

This book was a true friend—I wasn't going to be embarrassed about what it did and didn't do.

"That's the other thing about this book," I told the drums. "It's sturdy."

A VOYAGE TO ARCTURIS

But no one told me this when I was raising my son, when he was sick, when I was working frantically to heal his skincrust, fix his failing memory, his weak axles and wheels. I didn't know about Jaws or the dump until later—at first I was ordering all of my parts new, which cost me *hundreds of years*! Finally, when the VW was two and a half and sick as a forest, I clutch-cabled. I'd lost my job at the newspaper and wasn't making an income from my father's house, and I'd already sold everything I had of value: my banjo, my mountain bike, a few pieces of history that I wasn't using anymore (I sold all of my experiences with the Lady from the Land of the Beans one Sunday for an hour and a half, and a thief projector scene-talked me into selling the Cape Cod Wedding—fast dancing with the Other Side of My Mother—for a measly forty minutes.)

I had to do *something*—the storypumps were no longer accepting my promises of false future-time—so I walked downtown one afternoon and went into the store called Faces. I told the VW that he could look around as long as he stayed close, and I went to the counter and spoke to an old kiosk with a beard. I told him that I wanted to sell my name, and he laid it out on the glass counter. I remember how much he liked it, how his eyes lit up as he ran his hands across it.

I remember asking him, "If I do sell it to you, can I get it back?"

He grimaced. "Hard to say. Some of these names sell the same day," he said. "Others we can't *give* away. Tricky business, naming."

"This is only temporary," I told him. "Within a few weeks I should be finished with my new power, a road called—"

"Boy—what a *name*," he said. He wasn't listening.

"Anyway, I should be able to sell that route for a hundred-fifty, two hundred years," I said. "And then I'll be back for this."

Just then the VW spit up. I heard him retch and turned around to see him standing by a face-adjustment booth, his eyes receding in embarrassment. I went over and picked him up. "What happened, buddy?"

"I think I threw up," he said.

I looked into the oil and its images, spreading out on the carpet. "You OK now?"

"I'm tired," he said.

"OK. Just a few more minutes, alright?"

He nodded.

I went back to the counter. The kiosk was still studying the name—turning it over and over in his hands. "It's long, so that might keep people away. But who can tell? It really depends on what people are looking for. I can't make any promises," he said.

I nodded sadly. "I certainly understand the impossibility of promises," I said.

The kiosk paid me twenty-two hours, and then he took my name off the table and put it in the glass case. I remember looking through the glass and seeing it there, the sudden pang in my chest.

This was my *name*—my father's name, Old Forever's too!

"I'll be back soon," I told him.

That was so long ago. For years I castawayed and faithed, believing that someday I would save enough hours to go back into that story and slap my time on the table. "When they give me my name back?" I used to say, "I'm going to wear it like a Saturday."

But I'm no longer the person I was, and I know for certain that I'll never be that person again. I couldn't find him/her if I wanted to, even if I had a map of words to go by. The booking has taken everything from me and left me an integer, an underline, a noface.

There isn't a word on the planet that I would want to be called by.

VOLKSWAGEN DOESN'T STOP!

I can't say how far the four of us drove in that riff—how many chords or choruses, or how long it took—but I do remember that the night itself seemed to age. The starlit mountain-notes seemed to turn grey around the edges. The moon grew a beard.

I aged, too. Sometime during that riff my hair started falling off my head, and the skin of my hands softened and took on language-lines. My back slumped and my vision blurred. Was this the cost of my worry? My Fear of Death, translated? This was a different kind of learning—the attainment of knowledge that can only be gained from crushing loss after crushing loss. That fucking highway took *years* of time of money off my life, during which all of my memories were executed. Several choruses later, I woke up and could no longer see the edges of letters. Further down the road, an old Bean Woman returned to Northampton to visit me as I soured in the Northampton State Hospital—she put her hand on my knee and said, "I'm so sorry."

"For what?" I said.

"For this," she said, gesturing to the room around me. "For all that you've lost."

After she left, I looked out the window and I didn't even remember that she'd visited, or how we knew each other. I didn't remember *any* of the people that I loved—Emily, or the Lady Made Entirely of Stained Glass, or my brother, or the Two Sides of My Mother.

I forgot I ever even *had* a father.

• • •

I'm not sure how much time had passed—one hour or several—when the bioleggers and vegetables around us started slowing down, but soon the traffic was dirging and we were stuck in a noisejam. Inside the riff I was frantic, and I wondered aloud if it made sense for me to get out and run ahead on foot. The piano tried to calm me down. "I'm sure this will clear up soon," he said. A minute or two later he pointed through the windshield. "See? The traffic's speeding up over there."

It was true; in a distant moment, the bioleggers and vegetables were passing the obstruction and regaining speed.

We eased towards the source of the jam. The bass said, "What is it—an accident?"

"Fucking construction, probably," said the drums.

But I could see what it was: Something was stopped in the center of the highway—the cars were moving around it.

"Someone broke down," said the drums.

When I leaned forward, I could see a blue and silver shape in the center of the song. It appeared to have both wheels and wings—silver wings.

Tin wings.

No.

"What's—" said the piano.

No.

Inside me, a wave crashed on the shore and carried everything away.

"Holy shit," said the drumset.

"Is that—?" said the bass.

"No," I said. I said that word forever—I have never stopped saying it.

"That's a Volkswagen, isn't it?" said the piano.

"No," I said again.

"It is," the bass said.

It was.

The 1971 Volkswagen sat in the middle of the highway. The riffs and bio's that passed him were yelling at him to move and get off the song. But he wasn't moving—his face was dusked and he was completely still.

MASTER CYLINDER

I got out of the riff and ran over to my son. I screamed his name. "No," I sang, repeating the note over and over.

The VW didn't look like my son. He was retrofitted with tin language wings welded above the rear wheels, a shark-like fin fastened to the roof, and two external engines—one above each rear wheel. Smoke shouted from the engine compartment and my eyes whined from the smell of burnt words.

I opened the driver's side door and tried to start the car. There was no sign of life—the steering wheel was freezing cold, the dashboard completely dark. There were words *everywhere*. Every light and signal was at rest. I switched to another transmission and tried again to start it.

Nothing.

I checked his pulse. His engineheart was still beating.

My mind was a siren. First, I opened my power and looked through it for stories. The only one I had was a fragment, a crumble about a sveltbelt in the Land of Spelt who runs for local office on a campaign of dancing, and dances his way right onto the Board of Selectmen, and goes on to turn Spelton into the steppiest, most dancingest town in the Middle Way.

The story was flat and broken, but it was all I had and there wasn't time to book a new one. And it didn't matter anyway—I knew, even as I fed it to the VW, that his scanner wouldn't work.

"VW!" I screamed into the dark car. "Story!"

Nothing.

I grabbed a flashlight from the glovebox and got out of the car. The night roared in my ears and notes stung my face. I cut my shin on one of the tin wings as I sprinted around to the back of the car, and I shouted out into the song. Then I saw how complicated the new modifications were: He'd not only added engines, but two homemade *translators* as well. It was clear that one or both of them had overflowed or malfunctioned—the whole apparatus was covered with wordoil. And the wings and fin, I could see now, were connected to the new engines with flimsy midday cables. What was the VW thinking—that he could cut through musical resistance? Or that he'd *fly*? Did the VW expect less friction in the air of the song?

I opened the engine compartment. It was the inside of a diner now, but everyone inside the diner had been shot. The register drawer was hanging open and all of the blood from the victims' bodies was running together.

I closed the lid. The moon was dead, the mountain notes lying benignly on their sides and the stars sick to their stomachs, moaning and vomiting into the sky.

There was nothing more I could do here—I had no stories, no ideas—so I picked the VW up like I had when he was a newborn. With his wings and three engines, he was terribly heavy. I struggled to carry him to the idling riff; as I approached, the bass got out to help me. We put the VW in the back seat and I jumped into the riff beside him and said, "Go."

The piano pulled the riff back onto the roadsong while the drums and bass leaned forward to look at my son. His eyes were empty, his mouth was wide open and his skin had started turning grey.

"Is he—OK?" the bass said.

"Are those *wings*?" said the piano.

"Domino," the drums said, "that car isn't breathing."

"He has a pulse—his heart's still beating," I said. Then I tapped the piano on the shoulder. "Please just take us home," I pleaded. "57 Crescent Street, Northampton."

"We're on our way," the piano said.

I looked through the book of power, found a quick story, and tried again to scan it.

"I'm sure he's going to be OK," the bass told me.

"VW!" I shouted at him. "Story!"

"Can you connect the power directly?" the piano asked.

"Not without another morning cable," I said.

The drums sat back in his seat. "You know why he can't scan the story?" he whispered to the bass. "Because he's *dead*."

"No he isn't," I said.

Then the night said something, so I rolled down my window. "What?" I yelled to the sky.

"The percussion's got it right," said the night.

"His heart's still beating!" I yelled back.

"So what?" she shot back.

"So he can't be dead!"

"Would I lie to you about this?"

"You've lied to me plenty of times before," I sang.

"That was different—I was kidding with you then," said the night. "But your son is dead, ____. And your father, too."

IX. ENGINE OVERHAUL

The piano drove us off the song and towards home. When we hit King Street the drums told the piano to slow the riff down. "There's an oil-changery up ahead," he said. "Shouldn't we stop there?"

I shook my head. "That guy only works on bio's," I said. "I'm the only one who can save the Volkswagen."

"And why is that?" said the drums.

"Because he runs on *words*," I spat.

The drums huffed and looked out the window.

The piano steered the riff up Crescent Street and parked outside the house, and I got out of the car and picked the VW up. Then I stood beside the idling riff and I thanked the three of them for their help. "I'd still be running on the sidesong if it weren't for you guys," I told them.

"You sure there isn't anything else that we can do?" said the bass. "We can stay, and then if you decide you want to drive the VW to a mechanic—"

"He just said no to that idea," said the drums. Then he smiled at me curtly. "See ya, wouldn't want to be ya."

I ignored him. "The only thing that's going to save this car now is a good story," I said. "And I'm the one who's going to have to write it." The VW was getting heavy. I said, "I'm sorry for all the trouble we caused you."

"It wasn't any trouble at all," said the piano.

"Songs don't end," said the teary-eyed bass. "They don't ever end."

"And you?" I said to the drums. "Can go fuck yourself. The Volkswagen will *live*."

"The last note has rung, my friend," said the drums.

The riff pulled away and I walked into the house. Then I put the VW down, dried off the noted power, and started looking through the pages for a relevant how-to. I flipped past "Custom Modifications," "Runaway?" and "Word Breakaparts." Then I found the story I was looking for.

RESURRECTING YOUR VOLKSWAGEN BEETLE

CONDITION

The Volkswagen is dead.

TOOLS

- One charged book of power
- Spare morning cables, fresh and tested
- At least three plots

PROCEDURE

A lot of masks will tell you that the secret to the Volkswagen Resurrection has to do with the **engine**—with draining the **sufferoil**, finding the **heart** and reigniting it. That autologic is backwards, in my opinion; stories don't run on the heart, but vice versa. My theory on resurrections, therefore, is simple: You have to **write** your car back to life.

Every component has to do with motion—with converting stillness to change. If your car is dead, it's probably not a mechanical issue; it's more likely that the car is overwhelmed by something—by age, by sadness, by the noise of the road or the shouting from the city. It's this sense of being overwhelmed which leads to stasis.

The solution, then, is to tell a story which somehow maps a way *through* those obstacles—which clears a mental/physical path for the

Volkswagen, and encourages him to believe that there is **life**, and not death, ahead.

This theory is speculative, of course, and it drives in the face of what most "mechanics" say about resurrections. But my theory is that **belief**—belief as propelled by story—is what will start the Volkswagen and make his or her wheels turn.

Here's the go forward:

1. Design a resurrection story. In order for it to qualify, the story must include:

- A river or a bridge
- Something that seems dead, but is not
- Sunlight
- Frequent references to western Massachusetts

2. Sing that song. For example: A river travels a promise to see a dead Hadley, only it turns out that the Hadley is not dead—just very, very relaxed on a chaise lounge in the sun. It doesn't have to be complicated—it *shouldn't* be, in fact, because the dead car may or may not be able to scan it. If the story won't scan, try wiring the power directly to the dashboard. If *that* doesn't work, read the story out loud.

Several knots have written in to say that, heartbeat or no, a dead Volkswagen is a dead Volkswagen. But I don't buy that bread. Volkswagens are not born to die; they're born to speed through Northamptons with electric eyes.

3. Once you read the resurrection story, something should happen—the Volkswagen should open its eyes or say something. If not, see "Jump-starting the Volkswagen."

I began to write. First, I steered a story about the Bridge of Flowers in Shelburne Falls. The story was, the bridge seemed dead but was not—in the middle of winter it began to hum, the flowers chorusing and solving and sending messages. Then the sunlight began to harmonize with a song sung by flowers. Soon the entire story was a chorus.

I wrote all afternoon, replacing scenes and adding dialogue. Early the next morning, I wired the power to the dashboard. When the story wouldn't send I read it aloud, as dramatically as possible. "Soon the flowers began to sing in the snow," I shouted to the VW, "and the snow, frightened by the chords, gathered its belongings and caught the next bus East."

Then I waited for something to happen—for some sign of **life**. But there was nothing—not only did the Volkswagen not respond, he seemed more and more dead each minute. The scanner wasn't getting any power, the dashboard was quiet, and the wings had started turning a brownish-red.

I didn't give up. I wrote another story—this one about a bookstore in Montague, featuring books that are given new life and a healthy 1971 Volkswagen Beetle—and I read it to the VW. But there was no response to that one, either.

I spent four days booking—one story after another after another. I read each one aloud, and as dramatically as possible, but it just wasn't working—it simply was not the right strategy for resurrecting a Volkswagen Beetle.

In the end, I think the story of the 1971 Volkswagen Beetle would have been the same if I'd never written those stories at all—they didn't change anything!

And why, I wondered, had I expected a narrative resurrection to work in the first place? Just because I *imagined* that it would?

THE SHAPE OF JAZZ TO COME

If a montague won't get the VW running, maybe a castaway will. Let me just power up the power and see what it's sensing.

How about the sorrytale of the Castaway's mother, a wandering Sunderland diner?

No—too sad.

Here's one: a final-gear about my brother's homecoming.

Ahem.

That night I went home to my parents' house. When the VW and I pulled into the driveway I saw the Memory of My Father standing outside, watering the lawn.

"You see?" I said, stepping out of the car. "The color looks really good now."

"Not half bad, is it?" said the Memory of My Father, dressed in a too-small pink shirt that my father wore when I was a senior in high school.

"It's *morbid*," said the One Side of My Mother, sitting on the steps and smoking her fingers. "Fear of Death. It looks like a contract!"

I walked past her and went inside, where I found the Other Side of My Mother cooking in the kitchen and my brother watching television. He looked tired, and his hair was an apology shooting out in all directions. "What's going on, kid?" I said.

"Nothing," he said.

"Hanging in there?"

He didn't say anything—he just stared at the television.

The five of us ate dinner together, quickly and silently, and afterwards the One Side of My Mother complained to the television ("It's your *president's* fault," I could hear her say, and the television said something back) while the Other Side of My Mother cleaned up the kitchen and the Memory of My Father, my brother and I sat on the patio out back. It grew dark, and the plants crawled into bed and said their prayers.

My brother stared out into the night, his eyes wide. I witloofed him on the shoulder. "Let's get you out of here, man," I said to him.

"No, I'm OK," he said.

"Come on—it'll do you good."

"Where," said my brother, pool.

"Let's all go for a brew," said the Memory of My Father.

"Fuck it," I said. "Let's go to the Castaway."

So the three of us piled into the Volkswagen and we made the drive—up 5 and into Whately, past the Troubadour and Casper's and north towards the Castaway. Soon we were passing by the Antiquarian Book Center, and then we saw the pink lights blinking in the distance and the parking lot filled with cars. We pulled in, stopped, and the four of us walked through the heavy wooden doors.

Inside there was no room to sit; people were lined up against the back wall and huddling near the bar, watching a wheelchair in stockings on stage. In the corner, a band in leisure suits and derby hats mainstayed on a small platform.

The four of us angled towards the bar, sliding and pardoning, but then my brother stopped. "Oh shit," he said, and he grabbed my arm. "He's here," he visked, his eyes dancing.

"Who?" said the Memory of My Father.

"Colorado?" I said.

"At the bar," my brother said. He blinked and blinked.

"Where?" said the VW. "I'll kick his—"

"Shh," I said. I looked over at the bar and scanned it until I saw him. He was sitting on a stool next to a trailer park. The park had its lights on and the two were shoulder-to-shoulder.

"Who's that next to him?" I asked.

"His new *love-bling*," said my brother, his voice quivering.

"Fuck," I said softly.

"The trailer park?" the VW said.

I thought for a moment. Then I looked into my brother's face. "I'm going to go over there and talk to him," I said.

His eyes were faultlines. "_____, don't," Bryan said.

"You guys go over by the stage, get us a seat if you can—I'll be right over," I said.

My brother shook his head. "Let's just *go*," he said.

"It's a public place, Bry," I told him.

The Memory of My Father put his hand on my brother's shoulder. "Let's go sit down," he said.

The three of them turned and walked down the steps and I went over to the bar. When the trailer park saw me coming he whispered something in Colorado's ear and Colorado responded. The trailer park kissed him on the cheek, got off the stool and disappeared into the crowd.

I took a seat.

"I saw you," Colorado said, looking straight ahead. "I saw you guys come in."

I ordered a beerchai and a spider behind the counter moved to the tap and poured it.

"How is he," Colorado brusked.

"Not so good," I said. "He just sort of sits around the house."

Colorado took a sip of his mountainbeer.

"I don't think he really knows what to do next," I said. "He's pretty pauled."

"That's to be expected, I guess," Colorado said.

The spider put my beerchai in front of me and I took a sip. It was watered down and needed more ginger, but I didn't say anything. I looked into the beer and said, "I ought to debook you right here."

Colorado smiled and shook his head. "Make your try, commander," he said. "You've been getting your ass kicked the whole book—why stop now?"

I leaned towards him. "You think you can hurt me?" I said. "You could segment me, chew my face off, and I'll come back in the next story re-assembled and fullfaced."

"But still just as bald," Colorado said.

"Fuck you," I said.

The music in the Castaway was the sound of hammers being crucified, their lungs struggling to fill. We had to yell above it like a loan.

"I didn't mean to hurt him, _____," Colorado said. "I really never thought it'd go this way."

"He called me from the hotel that night," I said. "Told me every detail."

Colorado shrugged his shoulders. "So what," he said.

"Easy for you to say."

"It doesn't matter what he saw, or what he thinks he saw, _____. The truth is that I fell in love, OK?"

215

"My brother fell in love too, man," I said. "With you."

Colorado turned to me. "You don't think I was committed to him?" There was something furry in his teeth. "But he *changed*, man. He did. He lost that carefree thing he had going for him. Something inside him shut down."

"He was going through a lot. The Heart Attack Tree thing really unwheeled him."

"I'm sorry about that," Colorado said. "I'm sorry about the trailer park, about the old closed-down mental hospital, about all of it. I wish things had gone better—for him and for you."

"Please," I said. "Spare me the pity fork, will you?"

Colorado shook his head and looked away, and I took my beer in my hands and stood up from my stool. When I did, Colorado turned back to me. "Listen," he said. "Thanks for coming by. I mean it." Then he nodded over to the corner, where my brother, the VW and the Memory of My Father were sitting at a table. "Should I go over there?"

"I wouldn't," I said. "I think it might be good for him to work through this—to be in the same room as you and not have to be *with* you."

"Maybe you're right."

I nodded. Then I said, "Good luck with the park."

Colorado looked down into his lap. "Thanks," he said.

I leaned towards him. "And just be thankful that I didn't decide to rotate you," I said.

He smiled sourly. "Sincerely? Fuck you, _____, from the bottom of my heart."

I turned and walked away, over to the other side of the room, where the Memory of My Father, the Volkswagen and my brother were watching the wheelchair french a toaster. The Volkswagen was into it—he was standing on his chair, shaking his hips and yelling, "Go! Go! Go!"

The four of us watched for a while and sipped our beers. My brother seemed more relaxed by this point; he cradled his drink like a laptop and leaned lazily against the back of his chair. I was more relaxed, too. I was enjoying the rare opportunity to hang out with my brother and the Memory of My Father—the last one in the power, perhaps!—and the toaster's shiny surface was giving me just the slightest bit of faith.

But then I saw someone approaching us out of the corner of my eye, and I turned and saw Colorado—his monstrous legs, his cut-off shorts. He was standing there with a mountainbeer in his hand like an offspring of some sort. "Bryan," he said.

My brother turned and looked at him, and in that moment his face became an open dogma, a questionboat, a sorted screen of hope.

HI-PERFORMANCE MODIFICATIONS

I wrote for four days, with no sign of life from the Volkswagen. At the end of that time, when I had no more stories to tell, I brought my son to a bearded swordfish mechanic out by the state hospital. I hated the idea of consulting another mechanic, but I'd heard good things about this fish, that he was smarter than a lot of biofixers out there, that his time prices were reasonable, that he knew something about Volkswagens.

But when he opened up the VW's engine compartment he shook his head and told me that my son couldn't be saved. "This car is *dead*," he said.

"How can that be?" I said. "His heart still *beats*."

"Don't matter," said the fish, wiping grease from his fins.

"Doesn't his heart still hold stories? VW's *run* on stor—"

"Those Volksie hearts are sturdy as geese," the fish mooned, "but the engineheart alone can't keep the thing running. 'Specially with these modifications. Do you see what he tried to do here?" He pointed to the third engine. "He tried to *split* the stories. To reburn them—"

"He might have read about that in a literary theory book."

"It's an old, outdated theory," said the swordfish. "And see that translator? He was burning words in other languages."

I studied one of the wordcorpses that was burned to the VW's tire. "What language *is* that, anyway?"

The swordfish shrugged.

"Canadian French?" I suggested.

217

"Not to mention the fact?" said the fish. "That he's all rusted through."

"All *what?*"

"Rusted." The fish read my eyes. "Rust?" He pointed to my son's skin.

I shook my head. "I don't know what that word means."

"Listen," the swordfish said, crossing his arms. "I can't use the heart or the momentpump, but I'll give you thirty hours for the headlights."

"Wait a second. What?"

The swordfish's eyes were prairies.

"I'm not interested in selling the car for *parts*," I said. "I brought him here so you could save him. I'll give you all the time of money I have," I said.

"I told you, it's not a question of stories—he cannot be saved."

"Bullshit," I said.

"Sir—"

"There are still procedures I haven't tried yet."

"What procedures?"

"In the book of power," I said.

A wind blew across the grassy fields in his eyes.

"*How to Keep Your Volkswagen Alive*." I unhooked the power from my hip and showed it to the fish.

The fish flipped through the book and read one of the procedures. "You realize these procedures are stories—that they're fictions—right?"

"*You're* a fiction," I said. I took the book in one hand and the car in the other, and I walked out of that garage, down the hill, past the mental hospital where, before I was born, One Side of My Mother worked as a nurse. If people were confused or sad or frightened, she would help them.

She would *help* them!

PARAMEDIC

And then there was the time that I woke up tossing on the ocean. Somehow the Volkswagen had become seaworthy (with an outboard motor and everything), and I was now a captain, complete with hat. Where was the road? What changes had taken place to allow this to happen?

I have applied that question to several boats and frequent seas, but there are only so many words to choose from. Which ones shall I string together *here*?

I wasn't on the boat alone, of course—when I looked to my right I saw that there was a house in the seat next to me: a two-family, with yellow shingles and a bay window, on a quiet street near a crime-park. I knew this house well, could tell you every inch of it. At that moment, though, something was happening: Either the home was shot in the gut, or it was giving birth, or something—I couldn't quite tell. There was wooden fluid coming out from under its shirt, though, and it was breathing fast, and its eyes told me that a great deal was at stake.

"What should I do?" I asked it.

"Just keep going," the house said.

I pressed the pedal and we pushed forward on the sea. I took every turn that it asked me to. Soon it began to squeal with pain. "Just hold on," I said. "I'll get you there."

But I didn't even know where *there* was. I have never known.

And then there was another time, when I was driving with the Lady Made Entirely of Stained Glass and we put the VW on autopilot and went into the back seat, took off our clothes and made faith. And I'm trying to remember now if that was on the high seas as well, or if it was in the air, hovering oven-like over Northampton. But it's not clear in my mind anymore. People speak about memories as constant, as fixed, but my memories are films and the films keep changing. I've told lots of stories in which I'm driving somewhere with a girlfriend or family member in the passenger seat next to me, and even one or two where the car was filled with my friends. But in every one of those stories I knew—I have *always* known—that I was alone here. That I am the only one in this car. That the *car itself* will abandon me—that everything, eventually, will turn against me.

But you can *know* something—see it clearly, hear it highwaying all around you—and still not *live* it.

And I suppose that's what happened that day—that day on the sea with the Lady Made Entirely of Stained Glass. I feared into her, or killed her, and the sea responded, tearing into us. After a while, the turbulence became too much for the VW, and he became frightened and asked for help. The endless waves had nothing against my son or my girlfriend, but they—like the leaf, Bingo, and so many other Northamptonites—were relentless in their bookish hate for me.

So I climbed into the front seat and took the wheel, steering left and right, trying desperately to move us forward and to stay on course, one foot on the brake, the other shifting scenes, the VW swapping at the rain with the windshield wipers as the sea closed its fist around us.

There was still one procedure I hadn't tried yet. It was called "Jumpstarting the Volkswagen Beetle."

JUMPSTARTING THE VOLKSWAGEN BEETLE

CONDITION

Despite stories and swordfish, the Volkswagen is dead.

TOOLS

- A new believer
- At least one week
- One City of Northampton, including:
    - One Crescent Street, sunsung
    - A decemberchord Main Street
    - One chai-stocked Haymarket Café
    - A park for Pulaski

- The museum dedicated to sequential art
- The Revenge of the Fire and Water Cafe
- One pleasant Pleasant Street

PROCEDURE

You're here because you can't start your Volkswagen Beetle—because, at the end of every chapter, the disease of writing-in-the-blood won't bring him or her back to life. This is why many recommend the writing removal procedure; writing can be instructional, but it's not the end or the be. All it does is make time—and I say that as an author, as someone who makes a *living* with words!

In any case, the condition is: The Volkswagen is very dead. If so, the answer to bringing them back to life—the last and best option, in my opinion—is to jumpstart them. There are storysongs out there about jumpstarting with electricity—even transplanting the electricity from *another car*—but this is nonsound. If you were to really try that? You'd probably kill both cars *and yourself* in the process. Every car's language is different, so the translation would have to be exactly right, and it almost never is. Something is always lost or changed.

So I suggest a safer route: jumpstarting the car with *Northampton itself.* This is your book, after all, and all song long you've been traveling through a very particular set of cities and towns. We don't need a logic sweater to know that, if life itself is the problem, the energy and motivation needed can be found in those very cities and towns. See for yourself! Stand outside the BayState on a Saturday afternoon and watch all of the motion: the veggies and bio's traveling to Main and King, the joking sidewalks, the easthamptons and amhersts. All *you* need to do is create a situation in which your Volkswagen can capture some of that energy. There are stories and there is experience—there is the page and there is *life*—so I say, ward off Memory and jumpstart the Volkswagen with the effervescent rhythms of western Massachusetts.

How? Simple. Carry the Volkswagen down Main Street, Northampton, and let them smell the chai and remember the scones. Buy the VW a cup of coffee at Jake's, or a breakfast sandwich at Sylvester's. Your Volkswagen will remember that life is where it's at! And soon, he or she will decide to return. Because that's all living is: a decision. Breathing is a choice. Opening your eyes is an act of will—so is driving along Route 63, and taking a sudden turn onto 47!

And you never know when the VW will make that decision—when they'll choose Northampton. It might be on the bike path bridge, or at the China House. Your Volkswagen might be sitting there at the Florence Diner, perfectly dead, and then suddenly open his eyes and order a peanut butter and bacon sandwich.

I followed those procedures to the letter. The day after I read that how-to, I carried the VW down to Northampton Center and into the Haymarket Café. I ordered a cup of chai and set it on the table in front of him, hoping that the smell of ginger would revive him. When the chai grew cold, I carried him over to Kathy's for some eggs.

We were sitting there in the booths, though, when I heard the sound of a familiar engine outside. I looked through the window and saw a Volkswagen—the same Volkswagen I'd seen that day on Route 91—parallel parking outside the diner. I hadn't recognized him on the highway but now I knew who he was. I left the VW in the booth and I huffed out to the street. "Don't even bother parking," I shouted.

The Memory of the Volkswagen turned to face me. Its eyes were punchlines.

"Go—get out of here," I told it. "Go away and don't come back. This is not your home."

It silently sulked away.

When I got back inside our food had arrived. "Mmm!" I said to the dead car, "Eggs over-easy. That looks good, VW!"

But the VW would not eat, would not speak.

I continued carrying him around Northampton, to every place I thought might jumpstart him: the China House, Words and Pictures, Look Park, the Lord Jeff in Amherst, the Northampton Brewery, JavaNet. Everywhere it was the same—the same post-life quiet, the same stares from pedestrians, who were probably wondering why I was carrying a dead car in my arms, ordering it a salad or asking it questions.

As the days passed, I saw the Memory of the Volkswagen more and more. One day I took the VW to the Academy of Music to see a film and I spotted The Memory of the Volkswagen sitting in an adjacent seat. Another time, I was carrying the VW to Rao's Coffee in Amherst when I saw the reflection of a Volkswagen in a store window and realized that The Memory of the Volkswagen was following us.

I stopped walking and turned to face the Memory. "Stop following us," I told it. "Shoo. You're not supposed to be here." Then I turned and kept walking.

But the Memory of the Volkswagen followed us right to the door of Rao's and stared at us through the window as we stood in line for coffee. I ignored him and found an empty table. When I looked out the window ten minutes later, the Memory was gone.

After a few weeks of trying to jumpstart the VW, I lost one of the external engines one day while we were walking down the bike path in Northampton. I don't even know where I lost it—I just noticed that it was gone when we got back to the apartment.

A few days after that, I was carrying the VW to Florence when I heard a *clang* on the sidewalk and I noticed that one of the VW's wings had fallen off. I stopped walking, put the VW down and picked up the wing. By now it was all rusted and it smelled terrible, like forgotten words.

Something changed for me as I stood there on the sidewalk with that wing in my hand. It was at that moment, I think, that I surrendered. This procedure wasn't working—the book of power was wrong again. There was nothing more that I could do. The VW couldn't be resurrected and he couldn't be jumpstarted—no story on earth could save him. The VW was dead.

• • •

That night, I wrote one more story for the VW—a story of apology. I was the main character and the plot was, I was very sorry. Sorry for not taking better care of him. Sorry for ignoring the signs of his failing health. Sorry for writing the book of power, which had been wrong at every turn.

I wasn't listening, I wrote. *I thought I was, but I wasn't. I thought the stories would save you. That they would save my father. I thought they were worth so much more.*

And I wasted so much time! Time I would do anything to have back again.

No VeggieCar will ever replace you, I wrote. *All of my roadtrips will be* Volkswagen *roadtrips.*

Sometime that night, while I was writing that story, the Memory of the Volkswagen sat down at the kitchen table.

"How'd you get in here?" I said.

"Easy. I'm a Memory," said the Memory of the Volkswagen.

"Please go away," I told it.

"I'm not going anywhere, Dad," the Memory of the Volkswagen said.

ENGINE OVERHAUL

The next day I brought the Volkswagen back to the swordfish. I wouldn't look the fish in the face when I walked in with the car. All I said was, "How much again for the headlights?"

The swordfish crossed his fins. "Twenty-five," he said.

"I thought you said thirty," I said.

"They weren't so dusked then," he said.

I looked into his whiskery face.

"Twenty-eight," he said.

That day I sold that swordfish the memory coil, some of the morning cables, the passenger seat, the steering wheel, the dashboard and two transmissions. And whenever I needed time, I'd go back there and sell something else. Over the next year I sold him all of the transmissions plus the sound stage, the differential, and dozens of other parts. Some parts weren't worth saving (the fin, the second engine), so I put them in the dumpster behind the Crescent Street apartments. Other parts I stored in the VW's room; they're probably still there.

Every time I went to see the swordfish he asked about the engine-heart. I always declined to sell it. He offered me fifty-five for it once, then sixty another time. I shook my head and said, "The heart still beats."

"Seventy," he said.

"The heart of the Volkswagen is not for sale," I said.

"Seventy-five hours," he said.

"Not for all the time in Northampton," I told him.

X. KNOW-HOW

BUTTERFLY VALVE

These days, all I have left are these spare waltzes, sitting around and fermenting in jars. Like these over here, about the VW's experiences as an actor. Have I told you any of these yet?

I remember one time in particular, when they were holding auditions for the air-cooled play, *Emily Dickinson Rides Again.* The three of us—the Volkswagen, the Memory of My Father and me—went down to the Academy of Music one Saturday morning so the Volkswagen could read for a part.

When we got there we saw that the hallway outside the audition room was filled with other parents and children—baby lamps, small air conditioners, toddlers sitting cross-legged on the floor—but I didn't see any other Volkswagens. A spider came by and I gave her the Volkswagen's name. Then the Memory of My Father stepped forward and asked her to write his name down as well.

"What are you doing?" I said to him.

"Auditioning," he said.

"You have a role already—you're the Memory of My Father."

"I can play two parts at once," he said to me. "So can you, if you want to."

"But you're the Memory of My Father, which means that you're going to have to do your best to look and act like my *father*," I told him. "He would never audition for a play."

"There's a role in this play for the Memory of Mount Holyoke," the Memory of My Father said, and he flexed his bicep muscles. "And look— look at these guns. Are these things mountain muscles or what?"

"We've got a whole *book* ahead of us—" I began, but the Memory of

My Father flickered away, which he sometimes did when he didn't want to hear it from me. A minute later he reappeared in a far corner of the room.

In the end, I decided to audition too. I used to act as a kid, and I figured that I'd be making frequent trips to the Academy anyway if the VW was cast. An hour or so after we arrived, I was called into the audition room and told to take off my clothes. As I stood there, a man with a ponytail came in with two women and they sat down at the table. "Good morning," the man said.

"Hi," I said.

He looked at his clipboard. "That is a very interesting name," he said.

"Thank you," I said.

He sounded it out slowly: _____.

"It's French Canadian," I told him.

Over the next few minutes the three of them made various requests: They gave me a sandwich and asked to see me eat it, they asked how I felt about fences and they told me to read a few lines from the character named Tom, who was a General in the play.

"Tantamount *Price*!" I boomed, stretching my arms up to the sky. "Let go of my wallet, and let me seep into the night!"

I thought it went well, and when I spoke to the Memory of My Father he said he thought his audition went fine, too. But in the end, neither of us got a part. Only the VW was cast, and even he didn't get the part that he wanted; he auditioned for the role of the Volkswagen, but was cast as the Unforgettable Thermos instead.

After the parts were announced, the VW cascaded the director. "The Unforgettable Thermos?" he said.

"Of course," the director said.

"I read for the part of the *Volkswagen*."

"You did, I know," said the director. "And you were really very fine—you have a lot of talent."

"Then why didn't I get that part? I *was* that Volkswagen in there," said the VW.

230

"But you are so *right* for the Unforgettable Thermos," said the director. "The minute I heard your voice I could tell."

"*I'm* the Volkswagen, though," said the VW. "This is my story."

"You're *a* Volkswagen."

"Who's playing the part, then?"

"The podium's going to play the Volkswagen," said the director, and he pointed across the room at a podium, leaning against the wall and talking to a woman.

"You've got to be kidding," said the VW.

• • •

A few weeks later I went to see the play. I took the Memory of My Father and a half-faced woman who I was dating at the time. She was a real beauty, but we only dated for a short time because she fell in love with a pharmacy and left me for him. But we weren't there yet; things were still good.

The production was wonderful. The podium did a great job; he was the best Volkswagen I'd ever seen. His facial expression when looking into the dream, seeing Emily Dickinson for the first time? For me it held a real moment of growth, when a child realizes there are *walls* in life, places we cannot go. There is this world and there are other worlds, and pain blooms when we can see into those places, feel the need to get to them, and then find ourselves unable to, trapped in the here and the now.

The VW was good, too. He held still as the Unforgettable Thermos, he poured the sacred chai, he helped row the boat during the river scene. The lights reflected his blue, perfect face, filled with concentration. He looked, there on the stage, like a young milk cart in the making, and I was proud and filled with confidence for what he was and what he would become.

I reached for the hand of the woman with half a face, and I whispered into her one ear. "That's my son," I said.

I want to tell you the end of the story, the katydids raccoon, and I think I can do so in one seissun, a seissun I'll call "Know-How." Because now I know how.

The VW failed to track down the Heart Attack Tree, and so did I. Some roadsongs yield bookmills, and some trips trip and slip and break their Volkswageny necks. In the months after the Volkswagen's death I stopped writing about Trees, thinking about Trees, believing in Trees altogether. If I saw a Tree on the street or on a lawn, I would shout at it in disbelief and then turn and walk the other way.

I spent most of those first Memory of the Volkswagen weeks by myself, in my home, wearing silence and watching, through the window, the long, slow blink of Northampton—the way the city opened her eyes on me, closed them, kept them closed for a while, and then opened them again. I'd always ask her the same question: "Will you help me?" But of course she didn't respond. As if she wasn't aware of my sorrow!

"I'm all alone," I told her.

The city said nothing.

Sometimes, I'd forget the *How to Keep Your Volkswagen Alive* and I'd start driving out to Florence or Amherst just like I had six months earlier. I'd be moving at top speed when I'd awaken to the fact that my son, my car, was dead—that this trip was impossible, just a Memory. Then I'd have a breakdown-in-belief, which involved my stopping suddenly and falling to the ground, often injuring myself and ripping my clothes. Then I'd get up, brush myself off, and walk home.

But if you don't find the stories, they'll find *you*. And that's exactly what happened to me one Friday a few months after the VW's death.

By that time, I'd traded in enough of the VW's parts to be able to afford a used pair of BioLegs, and I'd gone ahead and had the surgery*. The bio's were slightly too small, and sometimes they really ached, but

---

* Later I would sell those legs for a few hours, which I used to buy a new intentioner for the Crescent Street house.

hey—they were convenient and reliable, and they got me from one chapter to the next.

I was short on time, though, so I was still selling extraneous chapters from the book of power. That day, I'd brought a few stories ("Valve Adjustment," "A Scanner Darkly," "Coal Miner's Daughter") to the Troubadour—an experimental bookstore in North Hatfield—to see what I could get for them. I'd turned in the chapters at the counter, and I was browsing through the shelves while the owner—a kind vinyl sofa—assessed them. I'd found a few books on the moment and I was skimming through them. Even though the VW was gone, I still had questions. I couldn't help but wonder, for example, whether Momentism, the belief system, had anything to do with a *momentpump*. So I was flipping through the beliefs, one by one.

Deep in those dark stacks I felt a tap on my shoulder, and when I turned I saw a tall, thick oak tree hovering over me. He was wearing a disguise—a fake moustache, fake glasses, a baseball hat, a trenchcoat—but even so I knew exactly who he was. I read his eyes and they told me the story. And I could smell the blood on his breath.

I'd always planned for this moment, for the day when I finally met the Tree, and how I'd hurt him in surprising ways—saw his arm off (how I wish I'd had my musical saw with me!), crush his face, poke out his eyes or kick him in the balls. But none of that happened. He put one branch over my mouth, picked me up with another branch and drew me inside his coat, close to his chest. Then he turned and walked towards the exit.

Inside his coat, it was dark as birth. There were stars, and a moon, and it was perfectly quiet. I couldn't breathe, and I didn't want to. I observed that I might suffocate, and for a few seconds every word was the same. I met my own Memory, looked into its hollow eyes.

The Tree rushed me out of the store and through the parking lot. When he opened the coat I covered my eyes in the new light. By the time I'd caught my breath and regained my wheres, the Tree was gone—I saw him sprinting down Route 5, the trenchcoat waving open to reveal his thick, barky legs.

I didn't chase him or call after him—at that moment I didn't even care about him. I was too stunned by what I saw in front of me. There, parked on a sidestreet about fifty feet away, was an idling Atkin's Farm.

I ran toward it as fast as my bio's could carry me.

HOW TO KEEP YOUR VOLKSWAGEN ALIVE *FOREVER*

The night had told me the truth about my son, but lied about my father.

He was sitting inside, heartless, at his table near the scarred window. He was only half-alive. His face was a still lake and his eyes were dirt roads. Through the hole in his chest I could see his lungs, struggling to fill.

"Dad," I said. "Dad."

He looked at me lakeishly. It was clear from his eyes that he had no heart.

"Dad," I said.

"What," he said. Then he said my name, and put out his hands.

"Stay right there," I said. "Stay right there, OK?"

"I'm not going anywhere," he said.

I ran back into the store and spoke to the sofa behind the counter. "Please," I sang. "I need to buy back some chapters."

"What chapters?" he said.

"Of the power."

"Which power?"

"The one I just sold you," I said.

"You sold it *here*?"

"Remember, I was just in here?"

"When?" he said.

"Five minutes ago!" I said.

"No kidding?" he said. "No, I don't remember that."

"Literally like five minutes ago."

"I think I would remember that." The sofa put his hands on his hips. "Well, I'll go check."

"Thank you," I said.

"Let me just find my glasses," the sofa said, wobbling into the back room.

Wires in my mind began to fray, to snap. "Please hurry," I said. "A man's *life* depends upon it."

Then I heard the sofa's voice: "Was it a book about sand?"

"No—it was about—"

"Was it a songbook?"

"It was stories from a book about *Volkswagens*," I shouted back.

• • •

I sprinted out of the store and back to the farm. I sat down beside my Dad at the corner table and I held out a story—a quickloom about a makeup named Emily.

My father looked at the pages. "That's supposed to save me?"

"It'll buy us a few more minutes," I said.

He took the story and began to read.

I got behind the deli counter of the farm, fired it up, shifted it into gear and sped it back to Northampton. There wasn't much money. I raced up the hill to the Crescent Street Apartments, ran inside, then coaled back into the farm and drove it out onto Route 5 and south, towards Springfield and the BayState Hospital.

Twenty minutes later I pulled into the hospital parking lot, parked the farm and ran into the emergency room. When the hospital recognized me his eyes became dry, dour stalks. "You," he hissed. "How *dare* you show your noface here."

"Listen," I said. I bent over to catch my breath.

"After singing the song that killed my son? I should have you removed—"

"We found the farm," I said. "And we found my father."

All his rooms were dark. "Good for you," he nickeled.

"But he'll die if you don't help me *right now*."

The hospital pursed his lips.

I put an oily, plastic garbage bag on the counter.

"What's this?" he said.

I pointed at it. "Look inside," I said.

He opened the bag and peered inside. "You must be kidding me," he said. He reached down to the bottom of the bag and pulled out the VW's engineheart. It was small, rust-free and still beating. "This is—"

"Yeah," I said.

"What am I supposed to do with it?"

"It still holds stories," I said. "A lot of them."

"A transplant?"

I nodded.

"You want me to—"

"Yes. Please. Yes."

His eyes were waiting rooms. "I should sit here and do nothing. I should let you watch your father die."

"Please," I said again. "I've already lost a son."

HEART SUTURE

TOOLS

- One engineheart
- Questionhope, one bushel
- One book of power
- As many stories as you can find

PROCEDURE

Do as much as you possibly can.

DIAGNOSTIC

I wish I could have shown you that engineheart—the system of pieces and parts that moved us forward, that moves us forward still.

One day, a few weeks after my son's death, I took the bolts off the casing and opened it up. Just to see how it worked. Opening that heart was like opening the first page of a book—there were characters (me, the Memory of My Father), there were themes (engineering, money, journalism), there was rhythm and chronology. I saw, in the images, old roads I'd forgotten—Huntington, Bird's Pit, Loudville—and scenes from stories where the VW was just a newborn.

I can't pretend to tell you how it worked. I tried to understand the science of it—the songs which ran from story to story, the small, multi-geared motors, the coils of wire—but it was too complex, too difficult to name.

But I do know that it held a true translation: miles to words, words to notes, notes to time. It was the *heart* that converted the pedestrian song of Northampton to something meaningful, and it did so via some sort of fusion: The turtle that howls a bluegrass tune at the edge of Bow Lake becomes a *warning* in the Volkswagen heart (Fear of Death + turtle = The Tale of the Fear-of-Death Turtle).

And that's just the beginning—the first heart layer. It will take years and years of study, and the energy of every single living thing, to understand the tiny minds and roads in the subsequent layers, the relationship between the music of one layer and the topography of another, the mechanics at work to make every single heartmoment turn together.

The world has *just begun* to understand the mysteries of the Volkswagen heart!

The point is, this *was* always the way it was supposed to be. Even I could see that the Volkswagen Heart was wired for travel—genetically coded, in this case, to track that untrackable farm. His pages were already written—as are mine and yours.

Yes, yours too! I am looking into your eyes right now and I am reading your life, and I am excited/sorry for what the road holds for you. It's going to be amazing/really difficult. You'll love/loathe every minute of it!

THE STORY

The surgery on my father took twenty-four hours, most of which I spent in the waiting room, floating in anxiety. Early the next morning, the Memory of My Father appeared in the chair across from me, studying the wall clock and writing notes on scraps of paper. After a few hours of waiting he said, "I'm hungry. Aren't you hungry?"

"No, I said, my body floating above the chair.

"I'm starving," he said.

Then he checked his watch, stood up and walked out of the waiting room. And that was the last time I saw him—he never came back from the cafeteria. He may be in Springfield or Canada, or he may still be waiting in line for hospital food.

A few minutes after that, a doctorcoat I didn't recognize stepped into the waiting room and called my name. I turned to face him. His coat had been white before the surgery, but now it was technicolored—he looked like he'd just been through some sort of colorwar, and lost.

"Good news," he told me. "The story goes on."

My feet landed on the carpet. "It does?"

"Thanks to the heart," he said. "Was that *yours*?"

I shook my head. "It's a Volkswagen heart," I said.

"But who wrote those stories?"

"I did," I said.

"The ones about Colorado? About Bingo?"

"Yup," I said.

"You know, those are some of the *loneliest* stories I've ever read," he said. "Have you ever thought about seeing a therapist? I have a colleague—he's very good. He uses a—I think it's called a therapy *machine*? So the therapy is very precise."

A few days later, after my father was restoried and speaking, I started up the Atkin's Farm and drove it to the old, empty site of the Cooley-Dickinson Hospital. I parked it there and left it. The farm stands there still, as a Memory-All for the BayState's son.

Now my father and I go there every Sunday. We sit at a table near the window and look out at the convenience store across the street and

the vegetables crossing between Northampton and Florence. I tell my father about the 1971 Volkswagen Beetle—about our summit-mountain transmissions and our bingo-bio-breakdowns, about the quabbins and the junkfarms and the podium productions. I know he probably gets tired of the stories, but they're the only way for him to know who the VW was—they're all I can do to keep the Volkswagen alive.

And he tells me stories, too—farmtales, mostly, about the Heart Attack Tree commandeering Atkin's up the Deerfield River, the Conway Inn telling anec after dote. Sometimes he'll be mid-adventure and I'll realize that the story he's telling me (a trip into Hatfield or Pelham) isn't his—that he never took that drive. He's describing one of the Volkswagen's experiences, a leftover in his engineheart, and he doesn't know the difference. But I never correct him or say anything about it. No matter who's telling it, I'm happy that the story is being told.

Every once in a while there will be some confusion while we're sitting there: An ambulance or an injury will step into Atkin's because they believe it's the hospital. They'll be bleeding, or screaming, or about to give birth. Someone will take them by the hand, lead them to a table and chair, and give them a donut. They will feel better immediately—they will no longer be ill, or pregnant, or in pain.

Here's how this works: At Atkin's, the donuts are homemade. Their outside is powdery, but when you split them open you find blood, and a heart. This, I know, is how everything works. Everything—the morning, the trees, every single page!—has a soft and plentiful center.

I have seen the future, and it is Atkin's Farm, where every road is a Route 47.

Oh God! There is so much to look forward to.

HARTFORD PUBLIC LIBRARY
500 MAIN STREET
HARTFORD, CT 06103-3075

Christopher Boucher was born and raised in western Massachusetts, and he received his MFA in Creative Writing from Syracuse University in 2002. He currently lives in the Boston area and teaches writing and literature at Boston College. How to Keep Your Volkswagen Alive *is his first novel.*